SAM(IRA)'S WORST (BEST) SUMMER

Also by Nina Hamza
Ahmed Aziz's Epic Year

SAM(IRA)'S WORST (BEST) SUMMER

Quill Tree Books

An Imprint of HarperCollinsPublishers

Quill Tree Books is an imprint of HarperCollins Publishers.

Samira's Worst Best Summer
Copyright © 2024 by Nina Hamza
Library of Congress Control Number: 2023943348
ISBN 978-0-06-302494-6

Typography by David DeWitt
24 25 26 27 28 LBC 5 4 3 2 1
First Edition

To Minoo and Muna, who know me best

Half Going, Half Staying

"Are you sure you're going to be okay?" Mom asked for the hundredth time.

"Definitely," I reassured her for the hundredth time.

Even though I was not sure.

And it was most definitely not a "definitely."

But Mom was already worried, and I didn't want to pile on.

She poked a partially escaped sock into the bag where the zipper gaped open, then sat on the suitcase. "I can still cancel this trip." She bounced a little to force the bag shut. "It's not too late."

Umma pushed the door open with her hip, her hands full with gifts wrapped in dachshund-and-Christmas-tree-covered paper. We don't celebrate Christmas and we don't have a dog, but Mom loves a deal.

"I didn't fly all the way from India to stay here with my grandchildren so you could back out last minute!" Umma handed Mom the unpacked gifts.

"I wish we were all going," Mom said, blowing away the hair that fell in front of her eyes. "Three of us going. Three of you staying. It's unnatural."

"We're going to be fine. Sammy will take good care of me," she said, draping her arm over my shoulder. I was already a little taller than Umma. "You worry too much."

Mom shook the packages near her ear. It didn't matter what was inside; neither would make it into the suitcase after the sit and bounce. "It's not you I worry about, Umma."

I knew who she worried about.

Zaara was starting college halfway across the country; after she came back from India, she would only have a few months at home.

Imran flipped out when his chicken nuggets were the wrong shape of dinosaur. The next two weeks of summer, while Mom, Dad, and Zaara were all in India, promised T. rex–sized changes.

But I was her worry for the summer. Even if she was too nice to come right out and say it.

"I'm worried about Sammy," Mom said.

I guess she wasn't too nice after all.

"Worried about Sammy?" Umma asked, pulling on my braid affectionately, her tone mocking Mom's concerns. If Imran dared to pull my braid, I would already have rewarded him with a revenge-flick right in the middle of his forehead. "Sammy is thirteen. She's not a baby."

I leaned into Umma's smell of jasmine and spices and her soft curves with perfect places for me to fit, feeling very much like a baby.

Mom smiled, even though her eyes were sad. "If I'm not here," Mom said, "I'm afraid Sammy will disappear from the face of the earth." Mom tried to sound like she was joking, but her voice was angular and sharp. "If I didn't force her, she would never join a single club." A worried knot of lines formed between her eyebrows. "If I didn't push, she wouldn't talk to a single person outside of this house."

She had nailed it. That was my exact plan for the two weeks they would be gone.

"Sometimes," Umma said, without changing her tone or missing a beat, "people aren't worth talking to." Umma could stand up for me without sounding mean or angry, one of the many things I loved about her. Since Umma didn't drive, there would be no theater camp, no public speaking camp, and best of all, no improv camp.

My next two weeks were completely planned out: I had an unread pile of books, playlists created, shows downloaded, videos that needed editing. My schedule was packed with nothing, exactly as I liked. Counting meals and bathroom breaks, and possibly combining both, I would only have to leave my room three times a day.

The first two weeks of summer were going to be perfect.

Mom threw the gifts on her bed. We visited India every year. Nothing went in after the bounce and zip.

"Plus we're going to miss your talent show, Sammy." She gave the suitcase a final pat before assessing me, like she often did, with her head tilted, eyes squinted, lips pursed. Like she was trying to figure me out. "I wish our flight was a few hours later so we could watch your performance before we left. I know how much you kids have been practicing, and I'm so proud of you for taking part."

I didn't have the heart to tell her I hadn't been to practice for over a week, didn't know if they were practicing without me, didn't want to be in the show at all.

That's what happens when you're signed up for a talent show with your ex-best friend.

Halloween in June

Middle school was a crusher of dreams.

I no longer had a best friend, and teachers assigned projects about dung beetles just in time to ruin weekends, and there was no recess, and my locker never opened on the first try. Not once. But middle school also made me dread the last day of school, the very day that used to be my favorite.

Usually I looked forward to our last day rituals: pancakes for breakfast, Mom and Dad's treasure hunt after school, and meatballs the size of my head at our favorite restaurant before everyone fell asleep on the couch watching a movie. Instead, I woke up on this last day of school with a stomachache and the sheets pretzeled at the foot of my bed. The worst part was knowing I had brought this misery on myself by saying yes when

I should have said no.

The sky slowly brightened and the silhouette of the tree outside my window came into shape. Something wasn't right. I pushed the curtain aside with one foot, knocking over two of my birthday bears. What I saw changed my day, my summer, and if I was being dramatic, my whole life. I tried to jump out of bed to get a better look, but landed on my knees when my foot got caught in the twists of the blanket.

Hanging from the branches of my favorite maple tree, covering the knot in the trunk where my toe fit perfectly, hiding the nook that curved for my back when I sat to read, were sheets and sheets of white.

I ran out of my room and leaned over the railing to see pots boiling and bubbling with no one standing over them, the smell of coffee already filling the house. I jumped two stairs at a time to where Umma sat on the floor, legs tucked under her, wearing the white head covering and gown she pulled over her clothes to pray.

Every time I needed an adult, they were praying. The faster I needed them to go, the slower they went. I hopped on one foot and the other, waiting not so patiently. She turned her head to her right shoulder, so I knew she was almost done. I barely let her turn to the left before pulling her to the front door.

"What's wrong, Sammy?" she asked. "Imran is okay?"

I pulled harder, wishing her legs could move faster. "Imran's fine. Imran's fine." I said the words twice so she would know they were true.

"Too fast, Samira. Your grandmother's legs too old." She always forgot the little words when we rushed her. The not-important words, she called them.

I opened the front door so she could see.

"Our tree," I said, in case she didn't.

The security alarm blared and Umma covered her ears. "Turn off alarm, Sammy! Quickly!" But I couldn't take my eyes off the tree.

Imran was yelling above all the noise, his bedtime cape crooked and trailing down the stairs behind him. Mom and Dad, in their pajamas with bed head and morning face, stepped around him to run past.

The phone rang, fighting to be heard.

"What's going on?" Imran yelled.

Umma stopped to kiss him on his forehead, as if there wasn't a siren, and the phone ringing, and things boiling over in the kitchen.

"No. Everything okay here," Umma said into the phone. "Alarm is accident," she yelled, too loudly in the quiet of Mom turning off the alarm. Umma handed the phone to Dad, who finished the conversation, and all of them moved to the front door, surrounding me in the spot I hadn't left.

Every one of us could see what had happened. But I felt the need to explain.

"We've been TP'd."

"TP?" Umma asked.

"Yes, toilet paper."

"I don't understand. Like decoration?"

"It's no decoration, Umma. It's a joke. A joke usually played during Halloween." Imran pushed through between Mom and Dad to get a better look. "Well, not joke ha ha, but a prank," I explained.

"Every year, Sammy, I ask you why people say trick or treat in Halloween and you say there's no trick, just treat," Umma said.

Mom and Dad walked barefoot into the yard.

"Maybe this is the trick?" Imran suggested.

Umma kissed Imran on the head again. She is the only person allowed, and took advantage of her privilege as often as she could. She stepped outside, lifting her white gown so the bottom didn't drag on the ground. The fake ghost to our June Halloween. Imran followed her. I followed Imran. All of us stood under the tree, the toilet paper hanging unceremoniously at various lengths. Some of the strands landed on Dad's head. Most of them were too high for us to reach.

Zaara joined us, her long black hair bouncing around her face, her lips outlined perfectly in light pink, her moon-shaped pendant matching her new blue dress, not a sign of sleep anywhere on her face. I stood next to her in my too-tight T-shirt from third grade field day, the one with a hole right over my belly button, my ankles sticking out from pants I outgrew years ago, hair from my braid escaping in all directions. It often surprised me that we were sisters. "Whoa," she said, looking over the tree and the toilet paper.

Even Zaara had no other words.

3

Not Even Toilet Paper

Mom was already grabbing trash bags, while I stayed rooted to my spot, unable to move.

"Imran and Sammy, get dressed for school."

We shouldn't even be awake yet.

"I want to take some pictures first," I said, clutching my phone. As official photographer for the school yearbook, I knew taking pictures was the best way to pretend like I was part of things when I didn't want to be. School dances, basketball games, and now toilet papering.

My phone blinked twice before shutting itself down. "I really need a new phone," I said, but no one was listening. Being the middle child meant a lot of hand-me-downs, and I didn't care about the patched-up snow pants, or the leopard-print bike helmet, but a new phone would have been nice. I ran upstairs to get the school's camera. Downloading pictures to my computer was a pain but more reliable than a phone that had a mind of its own.

I walked around the tree, taking photos from the street, from the side, from below the hanging rolls, grateful for the camera between us.

Dad jumped, trying to grab what he could reach. It was like a cruel game of keep-away. Not that every game of keep-away wasn't cruel. I tilted my camera to the top of the tree, capturing the toilet paper hanging at varying lengths, blurring and filtering the green of the leaves. Through the distance of the camera the toilet paper almost looked pretty.

"Why would anyone want to toilet paper our house?" Imran asked, breaking the silence. No one was ready to answer questions, but Imran was terrible at RTR— reading the room. When he asked guests how much they weighed or how much money they had, we tried to guide him back to more appropriate questions by whispering "RTR" into his ear, and fake-coughing "RTR" into our elbows. He never picked up on our hints. Never.

Zaara squeezed Imran, not letting go. He liked squeezes when he was starting to feel out of control, and Zaara knew exactly how hard and for how long. She knew before Imran did. He wasn't so easily distracted this time.

"Why would someone do this?" he asked, over Zaara's

shoulder. "I've never seen a tree toilet papered before."

I shook off the sheets that floated down and landed on my foot.

"I don't know," I answered, "but on Halloween, people TP houses for fun."

Zaara kept squeezing him.

"But it's not Halloween." Imran, always the stater of facts.

"Maybe it's because someone hates us." Me, always the stater of opinions no one wanted to hear.

I didn't like the look Zaara gave me. She released her Imran-squeeze.

"Why would anyone hate us?" he asked, twisting a sheet of toilet paper between his fingers.

"Sometimes people toilet paper houses because they think it's funny," Zaara answered, getting up from her knees. "They usually don't even know whose house it is."

"Or maybe they hate us because we're . . . different?" I asked, unsure if my question was Imran-fact or Sammy-opinion.

The paper in Imran's hands tore, and he let the pieces fall to the ground. "What do you mean, different?"

I swear it's like he's living on his own planet. "Different. You know—because we're brown. Because we're Muslim."

He pulled both sides of his cape around himself like a blanket. "So what if we're different?"

"Well, some people don't like—"

"No last day of school pancakes today?" Zaara asked, cutting me off, herding the two of us inside, quickly turning off burners with still-bubbling pots.

I watched through the window as Umma yelled at Mom and Dad. I could tell by the way she waved her arms. Those were definitely yelling arms. She pried the garbage bag from Mom's hands and shooed the two of them back to the house. Being able to boss Mom around is the closest thing I've seen to a real-life superpower.

They shut the door behind them, Mom closing blinds, Dad blocking the window.

"For the second time—go get dressed. I'm making pancakes," Mom said, opening cupboards, looking for pans Umma had already rearranged in a week.

"I don't know why you kids don't want dosa or idiyappam or something so good for breakfast, but pancake, pancake, pancake." Umma rambled on, listing all the wonderful South Indian breakfasts we could have been eating.

Imran dragged himself up the stairs ahead of me. His mood, whether good or bad, was always obvious in the slant of his shoulders. This morning his arms hung so low his hands touched the floor. "Move it along, Imran." I pushed him upstairs a little with my words, but more with my hand.

Too much had happened before seven a.m. on what should have been the best day of the year, and there was still the talent show, and half the family leaving the country to deal with. I leaned over the banister for a better view when I heard them pick up their argument.

"I don't think we should go," Mom said. "There are so many reasons not to." She moved Umma's pots aside for her pancakes.

I hardly recognized Umma's voice; she sounded like Mom. "Don't be silly. It's only toilet paper. I will clean up bottom and wind will take care of top."

"How about only one of us goes?" Dad suggested. "One parent for my brother's wedding and for Zaara to drop off the check, and one parent for Imran and Sammy?" Dad was always the compromiser.

"I could stay here," Zaara said. "I don't have to go."

Mom held her hand over the pan to check the heat. "You've been working all year to raise that money, Zaara. You definitely need to go."

Zaara sold T-shirts she designed to raise money for a school in India. All the students were on the autism spectrum and each shirt featured their artwork. What started as a simple assignment in one of her classes ballooned into raising ten thousand dollars, and she was going all the way to India to deliver that check in person. Zaara was practically an angel.

"I knew we should have all gone to India," Mom continued. "This was a ridiculous plan."

"We've discussed this so many times." Dad's voice was still calm, never the tiniest edge of irritation. "The trip was too much for Imran last year. He's not ready." The banister creaked under my weight. Last year Imran completely flipped out on our trip to India. He didn't like the smells, the number of people that filtered in and out of the house, the wrong kind of potato chips. Three days into the trip he stopped talking, five days into the trip he stopped eating. Seven days into the trip we came back.

"Maybe you forget? I raised eight children. I can take care of two grandchildren and turn some pancakes," Umma said, pushing a cup of coffee into Mom's hand and taking her spatula. "Whole family would be so sad if you weren't there for your brother's wedding. Tasneem even postponed her Bharatanatyam show for you."

It was all true. This trip had been in the making for a year. There were so many things that could have derailed it. Mom's worry about leaving me at home to do nothing but stay in my room. Their concern about Umma in America by herself. The pros and cons list Imran's autism specialists had made for them.

I never expected their plans to be scrapped by some toilet paper.

"Okay," Mom said. "We'll go, but tell us the moment something goes wrong. We will be back on the very next flight."

I knew they wouldn't have to cut their trip short. Nothing was too heavy for Umma to handle. Not even toilet paper.

A Valid Excuse

Thanks to international travel, toilet papering, and missed talent shows, all of us were emotional. I stacked my pancakes three high for added strength, and fortified myself for my parents' goodbyes by pouring extra syrup.

Imran went first. I watched my family through the window, hugging and kissing until the bus driver moved them along. My driver would not be as patient.

"I'm going to miss the Lego people he leaves for me on my bedside table," Zaara said as they came back inside.

"I've never spent a single night away from him." Mom was teary.

I waited for a pause in their conversation. "Can we say our goodbyes here instead of outside?" I asked, hoping they would understand. "My bus will be here in a few minutes."

"Of course we have to come to the bus stop." Mom was already moving into hug position.

"Uh, okay, I guess," I said. I had practiced in front of the mirror in my room, holding my head high, my shoulders back, making eye contact. But I crumbled immediately. I always had trouble standing my ground.

"Are you kidding, Mom?" Zaara to the rescue, as always. "The other kids will never let her live it down if they see her mommy and daddy coming to kiss her goodbye."

I mouthed a "thank you" to Zaara.

"Okay, fine," Mom said, already wrapping her arms around me, while Dad and Zaara waited behind her. I had that lump in my throat. The one you get right before the tears.

"And good luck with the talent show, Sammy!" Dad said. "I'll call the school and ask for pictures." I'm sure he didn't mean to sound threatening, but that's how I heard it.

Mom loved the idea of me being in the talent show. She was excited I was putting myself "out there." Luckily she would be halfway around the world when she heard I wasn't "out there" at all.

Umma brought me the paper bag I had purpose-fully forgotten in the closet. Without the wig and the costumes, I couldn't be part of the show even if I wanted to. The toilet papering and goodbyes had made me so emotional I totally forgot the bag.

That felt like a believable excuse.

I shook my head no to Umma, and she put the bag back under the hanging jackets.

Maybe summer would be okay after all. Umma was my sort of people.

Build a Bear, Lose a Friend

Someone was sitting in my favorite seat on the bus, so I slumped into the one behind. I had never spent more than a day without my family, and now I wouldn't see them for two whole weeks. I chewed the drawstring of my sweatshirt until it was soft, and pulled the hood over my head even though the day was already too warm.

A white blob smeared across my window, the bird who left the deposit nowhere to be seen. I zoomed in on my phone for a close-up, recording the short trail of white moving across the glass. I scrolled through clips of music before choosing something classical, with a loud drum. The seriousness of the music with the silliness of bird poop made me smile for the first time in days. I sent the video to the family group chat. Mom and Dad immediately replied with a thumbs-up and LOL.

The bird poop reminded me of Kiera, not only because it represented the kind of friendship we had by the end of the year, but because beginning-of-the-year Kiera would have loved the video. I knew nothing about what end-of-the-year Kiera liked. What she didn't like was me. I should have figured that out after my last birthday, but it took me all the way until Halloween. To what I (not so affectionately) call The Halloween Incident.

September 29 is my birthday, and every year since I was six, Kiera and I spent the whole day together, doing exactly the same thing. We wore T-shirts with photos of each other on the front, filled bags with candy so sour our toes curled, played mini golf and got clip-on hair extensions at the Mall of America, and finished our day by stuffing two small teddy bears.

"You're sure this is how you want to celebrate the day?" Kiera asked, on my most recent birthday.

"Of course!" I knew the plan was babyish and silly and we were way too old to be wearing matching shirts and stuffing bears. That's what made it funny.

The line for the Build-A-Bear store was out the door, and Dad found a chair and his newspaper. Kiera was antsy, looking over her shoulder, looking over mine. I thought she was excited. Turns out she wasn't.

"Wow. This line is not moving at all. You could change

your mind, you know. Do something else."

Change my mind? Of course we had to get the same exact bear. This would be my seventh. Seven was a lucky number.

Loud giggling drowned out the whining and almost-tantrums of little children in our line. The laughter was coming from the kiosk selling cell phone covers, and made Kiera's jaw tighten and shoulders freeze as she zipped her sweatshirt to her neck, as high as it would go. There was a group of girls and boys our age, a few of them wearing T-shirts with our school name printed across the front.

"Kiera!" one of them shouted. Kiera waved back.

"Oh no," she said under her breath, "they're coming this way."

"You know them?" I asked. I recognized some from history and PE. They travelled in groups, like flocks of birds and packs of wolves.

"Wow. Nice T-shirt," one of them said, pointing to mine. Today's photo had both of us in braces, sticking out our tongues, holding construction paper masks with feathers over our eyes.

"I know, right?" Kiera did that fake-laugh she only used when she was trying to cover her embarrassment. I didn't know when she had gone from my team to theirs.

"We're going to the jewelry store. Amy's going to try and get her nose pierced. You want to come?"

Kiera's eyes flickered from her shoes to mine, and back to her shoes. "You don't mind, do you, Sammy?"

Of course I did. I didn't want to spend my birthday at a jewelry store watching some random Amy put a hole in her nose. "Umm, I guess not. But we're almost at the front of the line."

Kiera flipped her hair over her shoulder like I had seen the other girls do. "Seriously, Sammy. You're too, too cute," she said, using the same voice she once used for Imran. She walked away with the Amy clan, easily absorbed into their crew. I hesitated a moment, looking for Dad to tell him where we would be. Kiera turned and waved. "Have fun with the bear thing."

She left me alone in line with five- and six-year-olds, wearing a shirt that made no sense without a best friend next to you.

But that still wasn't half as bad as The Halloween Incident.

I Think I Know

I usually loved the energy of the last day of school. We watched movies, stuffed ourselves with cookies and cupcakes, and teachers no longer bothered to keep us quiet. Today the noises clawed my brain like the sound of Imran practicing his violin, and the buttercream frosting soured my mouth.

I texted Kiera, typing, deleting, typing again, deleting once more. Kiera and I had been best friends since we were in diapers. When did writing her a text become so difficult?

I'm going to skip the talent show today, I texted. Sometimes simple is best.

Big surprise, she texted back. Sometimes simple can be mean.

At the beginning of the year we had moaned about

the cruelty of the scheduling gods, because we only had lunch hour together. Now I was grateful I only had to have my guard up in the cafeteria.

"Sammy, are you even listening to me?" Olivia asked, poking my shoulder. She had new rows of tiny braids for summer.

"Umm, yeah," I answered. "I was just letting Kiera know I didn't want to be in the talent show today."

She threw her dinner roll at me. "Yes! Does this mean you can take pictures for the yearbook? I'm off the hook?"

I threw the roll back on her tray. "Maybe." I had escaped one duty, and didn't want to jump into another.

I loved sitting with the yearbook club every day. They had rescued me when Kiera moved to a new lunch table. "Honestly, Sammy, we were all kind of surprised when you signed up for the talent show," Olivia said. The rest of them nodded in agreement.

I didn't blame them. I'm so obviously not a talent show sort of girl.

"Kiera," I said, as an explanation, my eyes darting to her lunch table.

"Yeah, I don't really get that friendship." Olivia squinted, waiting for me to explain. Her favorite part of working on the yearbook was the interviews.

"Kiera spends most of her summer in my neighborhood, at her grandparents' house. We grew up together." Olivia nodded, because forced closeness seemed like a reasonable explanation for our friendship. Kiera and I used to have fun together, running popsicle stands, selling cookies, starring as the sole performers in "Kierasampalooza," a lip sync we had created, produced, and performed right in my basement. "We used to have fun."

At the beginning of the year, bent over my kitchen table, heads together, we made plans to take our basement show to the school stage. By the end of the year, we weren't even nodding to each other in the halls, so I was surprised when Kiera waved me over to the sign-up table near the front office. "Sammy, today's the deadline to sign up for the talent show."

"I didn't think we were still doing that," I said. We hadn't spoken for months, so dancing together was not on my radar.

"You have to choose whether you're going to sign up for a solo act," said the man standing behind the table with a volunteer sticker on his shirt, pushing one clipboard toward us. "Or a group act." He pushed the other clipboard forward.

"If I want to sign up for a group act, I need at least one other person here, and they're closing down in fifteen minutes," Kiera said. That's where I came in. That's why she waved me over. I didn't have to say yes, but somewhere deep down, I was hoping she finally missed hanging out with me. Of course I was wrong. I was a warm body who could sign my name and I happened to have the right wigs and costumes.

Olivia poked me again, bringing me back to the lunch room. "Huh?" I mumbled.

"Can you believe the yearbooks aren't being delivered on time?" Olivia asked. "After we worked so hard to hit every deadline."

"I guess," I answered. I had bigger things than late yearbooks to upset me.

The rest of the table was more appropriately frustrated. I loved taking photos and the meetings after school, and having a group to sit with at lunch. So what if the books would have to be distributed a few days late?

I had been keeping tabs on Kiera from the corner of my eye, and pretended to laugh at something, sounding shrill and squeaky when I saw her walking toward us. Kiera's blond hair was pulled back in a high ponytail, with a few strands loosely framing her face. Her eyebrows were arched and thin, like she was always surprised. She touched the bridge of her nose, a habit she kept even though she no longer wore glasses. Her gang hovered over our table. We had started the act as two, until Kiera invited Amy to our first practice. Amy laughed so hard through our Beyoncé meets Beethoven mash-up, she invited Cynthia. Cynthia loved our Eminem-Bieber routine so much she invited Frank. I was pushed farther back at every practice and by the time we were at dress rehearsal, I teetered at the edge of the stage, almost falling off.

"Hey, Kiera," Olivia said, oblivious to the tension. Kiera wiggled her fingers in response. "Did you guys hear the yearbooks wouldn't be distributed today?" Was she still going on about that?

"I don't think I can be in the show today," I said, like I was reading aloud the text I had sent. I sat on my hands and tried to stop my legs from jiggling.

"You said. Soooo out of character." Her voice dripped with sarcasm. She turned to the rest of the group, pointing to the guy wearing a muscle shirt. He had an actual mustache. "He's taking Sammy's spot."

"Which one is Sammy?" Amy asked, looking over our table. She never got that nose ring after all. I had literally been with her every single practice, even sharing my hummus and pita one evening. She was a double dipper. Gross.

"She's purple wig," Kiera answered.

Umm, I had a name.

"We were hoping you guys could take some good pictures of us in the show."

Olivia nodded. "We always take pictures of the show." Then she remembered her outrage. "But what's the point when we don't even get the yearbooks in time?"

Kiera tented her hands on the edge of the table and leaned forward, like a villain from a movie. "With so many different acts, I want to make sure our yearbook friends pay special attention to *our* dance."

We wouldn't. Everyone who worked on the yearbook took their jobs very seriously. No one got special treatment. It was one of my favorite things about them.

I thought Kiera was done talking to us, until she turned around again. "Hey, Sammy," she asked, "what made you change your mind about being in the show anyway?"

"Umm, I don't know," I answered.

Kiera smiled.

The thought had occurred to me.

But I didn't want to believe it.

Considered.

And disregarded.

But I knew that smile.

I was pretty sure Kiera had toilet papered my house.

1

A Contest and a Favor

"Can I borrow Sammy for a minute?" The light from the open door faded the slideshow we were watching. I was happy to leave behind science class and the year-end roundup of frog dissection photos. "For yearbook discussions," Mrs. Markley explained.

She had a pencil behind each ear and bright pink glasses to match her dress. "Excited for summer?" she asked, as we walked to her room.

"For sure," I said. I was excited for this day to be over.

"I wanted to talk to you about a couple things." Her trademark hundred bangles clinked as we walked. "With all this yearbook stuff, I kept forgetting to bring it up." She unfolded a piece of paper from her pocket. "The printer was low on ink, but all the important information came through." The border was blurry and patchy.

"Young Filmmakers Society of Minnesota" was written across the top in faded green with parts of the letters missing.

"What is it?" I asked, even though all the answers were right in front of me.

"They have a contest every year. I think you should do it." She held open the door to her classroom. "Take a look."

I read through the details. The contest asked for three videos to be submitted. Each video should be no more than two minutes, and was supposed to highlight a different theme: My Home, My Community, My World.

"The deadline is in two weeks," I said, already looking for ways to say no.

"I know. It's a little tight, but I think you can do it. And I'm here if you need any help." Mrs. Markley never accepted a no easily.

I rolled the edge of the paper a little. "What does that even mean? My home, my community, my world. It's so vague."

"That's the beauty. It's open to interpretation. You can make videos about whatever those three words mean to you."

Teachers were always doing that. They say they're going to help but then make you do all the work. "I'd love to see you send in a submission," she said, jingling and jangling with every word. "I know it sounds a little overwhelming, but think about one video at a time. Start with the first one. Think about what 'My Home' means to you. Move on to the second once you're done with that."

My Home was currently wrapped in toilet paper. I didn't want to think about that at all.

"You're a natural, Sammy."

A natural what, she didn't say.

My mom is the reason I joined yearbook; Mrs. Markley is the reason I stayed. I loved the bright walls of the yearbook room, the smell of Sharpie and incense. Mrs. Markley taught me how to make videos even though videos were no help for yearbooks—she helped me with editing apps, resolution, aspect ratio. I was hooked from day one.

"The way you see things from behind the camera makes your pictures and videos beautiful. It could be a great experience, and who knows, you could even win."

I hadn't even decided to enter.

"Think about it. Now, coming to the second thing I wanted to talk to you about—I need a favor, Sammy." She jingled her arms wide, showing me the size of the ask. "Olivia mentioned you're not going to be in the talent show today after all." She paused for me to explain. I chose not to. "Their loss, our gain, because I need someone to record the show. What do you think? Don't hesitate to say no."

I wanted to say no, but instead I hesitated. Just like she told me not to.

"But we don't usually record," I said, part statement, part question, pointing to the yearbook covers framed on the wall, "just photos."

"I know, but since parents have to sit all the way in the back, Mrs. Carter insists we have video."

"Mrs. Carter? As in Kiera's mom?" I asked, already knowing the answer.

"Yes. She's head of the PTA. And she calls every single day." Mrs. Markley laughed to cover the annoyance in her voice. "You don't have to say yes, Sammy, but I thought it might be good practice for you, behind the camera."

I did not want to do this. Not at all.

"Sure, I can record the show. No problem."

Behind the Camera Is Not for Everyone

The gym buzzed with excitement; summer was just hours away. Hundreds of metallic chairs squeaked as everyone turned in all directions to have conversations with each other. Finally the principal tapped on the microphone and waited until the gym was quiet.

One stand-up comic, a gymnastics routine, and two piano players before *Kiera's Dancers*. I hadn't known that was the name that would be printed in the program. Like my signature wasn't next to hers on that clipboard.

"Why would anyone like being the photographer?" Since I had to record videos, Olivia was annoyed she would have to take pictures instead of doing her usual interviews. "You're on the sidelines recording things when you could be right in the middle, interviewing people," she said, nailing exactly what I loved most about taking pictures.

We waited for the stand-up comic to adjust the height of her microphone.

"I guess I like making people feel less awkward in front of the camera," I said.

Olivia finally realized the lens cap was still on. "I never feel awkward in front of the camera."

I always did. Whether I shoved my hands in my pockets or let them hang like noodles, my feet felt too big, and my smile was either Cheshire cat–weird or Mona Lisa–tight. "Well, some people do."

The comic cleared her throat. I zoomed in after she got her first laugh, when her nervousness fell away and her eyes twinkled with the excitement of being onstage. I loved catching those moments.

"When did you figure out you liked taking pictures?" Olivia asked in interview mode while we waited for the gymnastics boy to set up his mats.

"After a summer trip to the North Shore a few years ago." Dad spent so long trying to fit all of us in a picture with the lighthouse in the background, and when I couldn't stand adjusting and readjusting my massive feet any more I offered to try. "I don't spend a lot of time setting up, and everyone generally looks pretty relaxed in my photos." I even managed to fit the lighthouse in the back.

"So you're not in your own family photos?" Olivia asked. "My mom would freak."

The music swelled and the gymnast twitched as he stood at the corner of his mat, ready to start. "I use timers," I whispered to Olivia. But I had also successfully avoided many weird in-front-of-the-camera moments. People liked the way they looked in the photos I took and I liked not being in them. Win-win.

The boy with the gymnastics routine stuck his landing. Olivia waited for him at the bottom of the stairs to get her interview even though that wasn't her job for the afternoon.

Standing behind the camera isn't for everyone.

When the second piano player bowed, Kiera's group took the stage. She was in the middle, the others surrounding her. She was always more comfortable onstage than me. If I'm being honest, she was always more comfortable offstage than me as well.

Three Observations; Three Realizations

I noticed some things immediately—three observations.

I figured out some things right after—three realizations.

Observation #1: Costumes. They were not the ones we had agreed on. The dancers were wearing shawls and kurtas and skirts with Indian mirror work. The bag with a boa and fedora still sitting in my coat closet would have been useless even if I had "remembered."

Observation #2: The music. This was most definitely not Beyoncé. Unlike most people in the gym, I recognized these Bollywood songs.

Observation #3: The dance moves. None of the moves were the ones we practiced. Instead, Kiera performed an exaggerated version of dance steps from Hindi movies she and I had grown up watching in my basement. The others danced around her, twirling shawls in the air like they were at a rodeo. I had never been a fan of those movies, but Kiera loved them. Or I thought she did.

Realization #1: They had been practicing without me. They hadn't canceled practice, what they had canceled was me.

Realization #2: They were making fun of Indian music and Indian dance moves. This was not a dance in support and appreciation of Bollywood. This was a spoof. They could barely stifle their giggles. "I'm laughing with you, not at you," Kiera would have said. Whenever she said that, I knew the opposite was true.

Realization #3: No one was going to stop them. Not the teachers, who had no way of knowing this was a spoof, not the parents, who were probably pleased to see the school welcoming different cultures, and most definitely not me, hiding behind the camera.

My face flushed, but I wasn't angry. I was embarrassed. Then I was angry at myself for being embarrassed.

"Shouldn't you be recording?" Olivia asked, half-heartedly clicking pictures.

"Umm, yeah." I started to record, not wanting to let Mrs. Markley down. Letting myself down in the process.

Their act wasn't funny, their timing was off, their costumes were pathetic. The only people laughing were the ones onstage. If I hadn't decided to quit the dance, how long would it have taken me to realize I was in the wrong costume doing the wrong moves? That would have given everyone something to really laugh about.

I couldn't understand why my face was hot, why my hands shook. No one knew I had been cut from the dance on purpose, or that being Indian was the butt of their joke. And I wasn't the one boring the audience.

If I were my mom, I would have made the dancers stop. If I were Zaara, I would have found a teacher and explained. If I were Imran, I would have yelled something loud and obnoxious right in the middle of their performance.

But I'm not.

Instead I stuck my finger across the lens to block most of their act. Did that make me feel better? I wish I could say no.

10

Secret Weapon

This had been one of the longest days of my life, and I willed the bus to go faster so I could get to my room and possibly never leave. I squeezed my eyes together, blurring the red of the traffic light. Front yard that needed to be cleaned, toilet-papered tree—out of focus was my favorite way to see things I didn't want to deal with.

My head hit the seat when the driver slammed the brakes; every stop was a surprise for him. I missed the last step off the bus, almost falling victim to my self-induced blurriness. I opened one eye cautiously, and then the other. The tree was mine again. There was no toilet paper. None on the grass, none on the branches, none hanging from the nest at the very top.

"How'd you do it, Umma?" I asked, dumping my

backpack in the mudroom, wishing I could dump my feelings from the day as easily.

"Oh, I am very, very cold," Umma said, snapping her fingers. She meant she was cool, but I didn't correct her. When someone's English is a little "broken," as Umma called hers, they could probably speak circles around you in another language or two. Umma spoke five languages and was always the smartest person in the room.

"But how'd you get to the very top of the tree? It's like twenty feet high!"

"My secret weapon," Umma said, showing me her cell phone. I had nicknamed her phone "the secret weapon" on our last trip to India because Umma could fix any problem with a few well-placed calls.

"Your secret weapon works in the US?" I asked.

She shrugged and nodded at the same time like it was no big deal.

If I was going to make videos for the film competition, and I most definitely was not, her secret weapon would be part of "My Home." In India, her secret weapon summoned a bowl of hot mac and cheese when I missed American food, and got us tickets to sold-out concerts.

"You called someone in India and they fixed the tree all the way here?" I asked, taking a video of Umma holding up her secret weapon, on the very slight chance that

I decided to submit a video. Umma was very much an in-front-of-the-camera person.

"Of course not," she said laughing. "Dana's grandson got a new job. Finally, something he likes. So many wrong jobs first. Now he works fixing electricity lines."

I didn't know what to ask first.

"And that helped clean up our tree?"

"He drives one of those trucks, with a basket that can go up and up so he could reach all the way to top."

I didn't know what to ask next.

"And who is Dana?"

Umma already had a pan of oil heating on the stove and dropped in the first samosa. The test samosa.

"Oh, I can't remember last name. I met her when I go for my walk. Very nice lady, old like me, my height, short spiky blond hair, always smiling face." She stuck her fingers up from the top of her head replicating spikes of hair.

The samosa sizzled, and Umma pushed it around the oil.

"Mrs. Richardson?" She was the only one I knew with spiky hair, but the rest of her description didn't make sense. She was much taller than Umma and I didn't think I had seen her smile once. Not when she handed out raisins when we went trick-or-treating, and not when

Kiera and I used to pull weeds for her. Always a scowl, never a smile.

"That's right! Richardson." She scooped the samosa out and dropped it on the plate lined with a paper towel to soak up the oil.

"And you know her grandson?"

"Pete? Wonderful boy. This job will be much better. He can still have time to practice with his band."

"Pete's in a band?" I hadn't known she had a child, let alone a basket-riding, band-practicing grandson.

"He's very good at electric guitar. But not as good as Billy on the little piano thing. He listen to my ghazal one time and he can play the same tune right away. Amazing."

What was even happening?

"You met the whole band, Umma?" She poured Hot & Sweet ketchup next to the samosas, but I was still soaking in the information.

"Lovely boys. They cleaned up the whole toilet paper so quickly." She snapped to show how fast.

"How do you know all those people already, Umma?"

"Well, you know back home, every morning Bappa and I would talk to all the neighbors?" My grandfather passed away a few years ago. Umma's voice still caught in her throat when she talked about him. "No one visits each other in the mornings here. I made snack in morning and waited for someone to come over with their cup of tea and talk. No one came, so I go to their houses." She pushed the plate closer to me.

The samosa was hot and I tossed it from hand to hand. "People don't do that here, Umma. It's kind of weird. You don't drop by without letting them know."

"You're right. Only first day. Now Mrs. Richardson leaves her front door open waiting for me. And not only her."

I couldn't imagine going anywhere without an invitation, let alone to scowl-faced, raisin-distributing Mrs. Richardson's. Umma didn't speak English very well, she wore sarees, she had only been to the US a few times, and none of that bothered her.

"Your Umma pretty cold, right? I say that right? I get things done."

"The word is 'cool,' Umma." And I nodded. Because she was.

"Cool like you, Sammy. You and me are both so same."

We were not. But I liked the sound of the words and didn't bother to correct her.

11

A Little Lie for Imran

Standing outside, the sun shining, the toilet paper completely cleaned up, the last day of school behind me, I could pretend like the day never happened. I reminded myself that at least I wouldn't have to see Kiera for the next three months. I waited for Imran's bus, because that's the kind of thing Zaara would do. I was the go-to sister now. Well, the only sister. I would have to step up.

His shoulders drooped so low his knuckles almost grazed the ground, and he dragged his backpack behind him, smudging part of the first clue Mom and Dad had chalked on the driveway. The message was written using semaphore flag signals. Imran was an expert, and the only reason anyone in our family knew the word *semaphore*.

"Hey, Imran! Last day of school. Woo-hoo!" I pretended excitement for him.

"Did Mom and Dad call? Did Zaara?"

I was lowest on the rung of people he counted on. My step-up was steeper than I realized.

"They're still traveling." I pointed to the sky. "They can't call." I stepped to the side of the driveway to point out the stick figures holding square flags. "Look Imran, the first clue." He loved a good coded message.

The treasure hunt, the flag signals, Imran's slopy shoulders. That could be a single shot for the video about "My Home." I hadn't decided one way or another, but the perfect shots kept creeping into my head.

"I can't stop thinking about the toilet paper," he said. Usually coded messages made him salivate. "I mean, why would someone do that?" He didn't mention the cleaned-up tree.

"It's not a big deal, Imran. Don't think about it." That's like telling someone to relax or be patient. Or think about anything other than Kiera toilet papering your house.

Umma looked tiny, standing in the front door still wearing the apron that almost reached her ankles, the one with the Eiffel Tower on the front. It was too big for anyone in the family and none of us had been to Paris.

"Shall we go on treasure hunt, monay? Your mom kept everything close to home so I could walk with you."

"I'm not really in the mood, Umma."

Zaara would be hugging him now, holding him tight. I'm not much of a hugger.

"Then both of you come inside. I made murukku and I have Marie biscuits for you to dip into the chaya. Maybe after snack you'll feel like doing treasure hunt."

Slopy-shouldered Imran might not recover from a biscuit falling into his tea, dipped a moment too long. "Imran loves murukku, Umma. Today doesn't feel like a biscuit sort of day."

Crisis averted.

He hung his head in his hands over the cup of tea, not touching his plate.

"Someone sneaked up in the middle of the night and threw toilet paper at our house because we're Muslim and because we're brown?" I understood why Zaara had given me the stink eye when I planted that idea for Imran. She knew it would take root. "It doesn't even make sense. I asked every single person in school today if their house had ever been toilet papered." When Imran says every single person, he means Every. Single. Person. "What does toilet paper have to do with being brown anyway?" he asked.

I bit into another samosa to buy time. I didn't want to tell him Kiera was probably the one who toilet papered the house. Besides, I didn't know for sure. And I didn't want to answer the million questions that would come after. I chose to distract him instead.

"You know we weren't the only ones, right?" I lied. Zaara had told me a million times to not lie to Imran, that the truth only hurt worse later. I had been primary big sister for less than an hour and I was already messing with the rules.

His shoulders immediately lifted a tiny bit. That's the thing about Imran, shoulders easily down and easily lifted.

"Yeah. Mrs. Richardson's house down the street got TP'd too." Mrs. Richardson and her grandson were still on my mind since Umma's conversation.

"Really?" Shoulders higher.

"Oh yeah, big old mess of toilet paper over there too," I added.

Shoulders at his ears. "Let's go see."

I may have gone too far. Umma stopped humming mid-tune, and they both waited for my answer.

"Well," I said, dragging my words out slowly, "her mess is all cleaned up. Mrs. Richardson's grandson is the one who helped clean ours too."

"Pete?" Imran asked, swinging his legs, kicking the cupboards under the kitchen island in a steady beat.

Was I the only one who didn't know Pete?

"Why would someone TP *his* house?" Imran asked.

I blocked his kicking legs with my foot, stopping the thuds. "How would I know that?" I asked, annoyed with Imran's questions when I was trying to help him.

He broke off a piece of murukku but left it on the plate. "I don't know." His voice lost its enthusiasm. "I was just asking."

"Actually," Umma said, turning the stove on again, to heat the oil, "Pete thinks it's a prank, like Sammy said." Umma lied with a straight face. Apparently she was ignoring Zaara's rules about lying to Imran as well. "They spent so much time cleaning our tree, their toilet paper is still there." She opened cupboards to find the right plate. "Let me fry some samosas to take, and then we can go see. Dana loves Indian food."

"Oh good," Imran said, jumping out of his seat.

"I'll come too," I said. I would have to collect all the abandoned treasure hunt clues, but first I needed to see how Umma was going to pull this off. Spending the first two weeks of summer in my room could start tomorrow.

Captain Butt-Crack and the Wrong-Sized Bike

Imran dug through the basket under the TV, looking for his cape with letter *A* stitched on the back. Capes were only one of his many current obsessions.

"I will pray, and then we can go," Umma said, confirming my theory that prayers happened only when I had no patience for them. I would have to include Umma and her prayer mat for the "My Home" video. If I was going to make a video. Which maybe I would.

I carried the plate of samosas, covered in aluminum foil, and Imran led the way on his scooter, circling back when he got too far ahead. He liked to watch the shadow of his cape lift and drop. I was surprised he didn't crash into something.

At the end of our street, where the road curved and

changed direction, I craned my neck to see how Umma had fixed the problem. I knew, without a doubt, that Mrs. Richardson's house hadn't been toilet papered. But Umma was going to make it happen, and I wanted to see how. A white moving truck was parked in the middle of the road, blocking our view.

"I didn't know someone was moving in," Umma said.

"Or out," I replied.

A man with his baseball hat on backward, wearing a T-shirt that used to be white with "Best Movers" written across the front in cursive, rolled two bikes out of his truck. One would have been the perfect size for me. Mom would already be at their front door arranging a "play date" and apologizing for my shyness.

Imran slowed his scooter to a stop in front of the other mover, the one whose T-shirt rode up exposing half his butt.

"Helloooo, Captain Butt-Crack," Imran said.

I waited for Butt-Crack's response. When Imran was a little too honest with strangers, the best thing to do was wait. Sometimes they'd find his honesty hilarious and we'd be okay, but sometimes they would be angry and we would have to apologize. I saw Butt-Crack's face turn red. This could go either way. He had one of those loud laughs, the kind that echoed through the neighborhood.

Thank goodness. Imran was already moving past him, ready to insult the next person.

"What's the 'A' for?" Butt-Crack asked, pointing to Imran's cape with one hand, pulling his jeans up with the other.

This could go one of many ways as well, depending on Imran's mood in the moment.

"Wait, wait, let me guess," Butt-Crack said, cupping his chin. "Captain Awesome?"

Imran shook his head.

"Captain Amazing?"

Imran shook his head again.

"Captain Armpit?"

That, of course, got Imran to chuckle. He was always a sucker for the cheap laughs.

"We've got a whole truck to unload. Get to work," growled backward-hat guy, lifting one side of a green velvet couch.

Imran flexed both arms, letting his scooter fall to the ground. "Captain Autism," he said.

Butt-Crack winked at him. "I've got to admit, I did not see that one coming."

Most people don't. Mom and Dad told Imran there was a chance Galileo and Einstein were on the spectrum. Now Imran thought autism was a superpower, confirmed by the cape Zaara had made for him.

"Who is moving in?" Umma asked.

"A mom and daughter combo," he said.

I hoped the daughter wasn't my age. Maybe the size lied, and this was a bike she was waiting to grow into, or one she had already grown out of.

"Lucky you. The girl looks about your age," he said.

I hadn't asked.

"I bet they like Indian food," Umma said to no one.

A Different Sort of Toilet Papering

Past the moving truck, Mrs. Richardson's front lawn came into view. Every house was similar, with white slats and brown sloping roofs, but different because of the chairs on the front porch, planted flowers, and whether your tree had been toilet papered or not.

"Where's the toilet paper?" Imran asked. A very valid question.

"Hmm," Umma said. "Maybe they cleaned up early?" She made her way to the front door. "Let's ask."

Covering the wood planks of Mrs. Richardson's front porch was the toilet paper we were looking for.

"I found it," Imran squealed, like the rest of us hadn't.

The paper was laid out in precise rows. Only the few sheets covering her potted plant looked out of place. We hesitated at the bottom of the steps, not ready to disturb the neatness. Ours was chaotic, in the open, at the top of the tree and impossible to hide. Mrs. Richardson's was laid out like a large welcome mat while ours was a sign to go away.

Her perfect sheets of white in contrast to my photos of our messy tree could make a great scene.

"Who wants to ring the bell?" Umma asked.

Imran climbed the stairs delicately, on his toes, not wanting to destroy the pristine, white, newly laid carpet of toilet paper. He rang the bell and followed his footsteps back toward us, like we did when we got the newspaper in freshly fallen snow. We were quiet as we waited for Mrs. Richardson to answer the door, each of us considering explanations for this strange version of toilet papering.

"Can you believe this mess?" Mrs. Richardson asked as she opened the door, frowning, not smiling. Exactly as I remembered. "I can't imagine who would want to play such a silly prank on me."

"Wellllllll," Imran said, measuring his words. Pausing to think before speaking wasn't a common occurrence for him. "It's not really like ours. Yours is super . . . organized."

"Oh really?" Mrs. Richardson said, stepping on her white paper carpet, ruining the perfection. "Toilet paper goes in the house, not on the front step. What's organized about that?"

"I gueeeeeeess," Imran replied.

"Yours was toilet paper. Mine is toilet paper. Yours is outside your house. Mine is outside my house. You don't know who did yours. I don't know who did mine. The only difference is that yours is in the tree and mine is at my front door. Isn't much of a difference, if you ask me."

"Hmm," Imran said, and we waited while he decided how he felt. "I guess you're right."

Phew. I didn't know what my next move was going to be if this hadn't worked.

"I made you some samosas," Umma said, handing over the plate. "You like Indian food, right?"

"I do." Mrs. Richardson lifted the foil that had changed color with the warmth inside, and inhaled. "Thank you."

"Thank *you*," Umma said. Mrs. Richardson and I knew what she was being thanked for. "You have new neighbors moving in?"

"Yes. Betsy's daughter and granddaughter are moving in for a while."

Imran started to make little piles of toilet paper with his toe.

"You're lucky, Sammy," Mrs. Richardson said. "I think she's about your age."

Everyone was suddenly obsessed with my age.

"You want to come in for a bit?" she asked, pointing her plate of samosas at her front door.

Luckily Imran was already tugging at Umma's sleeve

to leave. "Another time. Their parents will be calling soon."

Mrs. Richardson's usual pinch-faced scowl was replaced by disappointment that we weren't staying. "I heard Zaara is going away to college this year, that she wants to be a doctor. You must be very proud."

"Yes, proud of all my grandchildren," Umma said, squeezing us close. "And Zaara is so happy. She always wanted to be doctor."

Not true at all. Maybe when she was six, when I wanted to be a firefighter, like Imran wants to be Spiderman. I knew Zaara didn't want to be a doctor, but she polite-smiled and polite-nodded every time someone proudly mentioned medical school.

"I'll send the kids over tomorrow to clean up the front step," Umma said, allowing herself to be dragged away by Imran.

"Don't worry about that. I can clean up," Mrs. Richardson said. "It won't take long."

"You rest up for your surgery," Umma yelled over her shoulder. "Kids will clean up tomorrow, before the rain."

I guess I knew what I would be doing the next day. Not hanging out in my room. The perfect summer would have to wait one more day.

From Bad to Worse

I woke up to rain lightly tapping my window, bad weather confirmed by swirls of wind and bolts of lightning on my weather app. If I waited for Imran to choose the perfect cape and pick out all the rainbows from his bowl of Lucky Charms, we would be cleaning up wet toilet paper scattered by the wind.

I dressed quickly and texted Umma, passing Mom and Dad's dark room and Zaara's closed door on the way downstairs. I had never stayed in the house without them and was happy to see Imran's solar system night-light glowing under his door.

I gripped the plastic bags tightly around the handle-bars, but they still filled with air, and my knees knocked them from side to side with every turn of the pedals. I leaned my bike against the house gently and tiptoed to the front door. I didn't want Mrs. Richardson to hear me and start awkward conversations about my favorite subject in school. I crouched uncomfortably on the porch, one knee holding down a bag being whipped side to side while I tried to scoop the wet, heavy toilet paper inside. I tried to take a quick shot with my phone when a sudden gust filled the bag, carrying it down the driveway. I was not off to a good start. I zigged and zagged after the bag until it stopped, caught around the front wheel of a bike. The same red bike from the moving van yesterday, belonging to the girl Mrs. Richardson and Captain Butt-Crack thought I'd want to be friends with. I sized her up. They were right about her being my age.

She peeled the bag off her bike wheel, fighting a little against the wind, and held it in the air triumphantly, like a trophy, the other hand waving wildly until I was shamed into waving back.

"Hey, I'm Alice. And I come victorious!" she said, still holding the bag over her head, star-shaped white sunglasses protecting her from the zero sun. She pushed the glasses to the top of her head. Her big green eyes were bright against her red hair. She had a crinkle above her nose and a wide smile—the kind of face where everything seemed to fit perfectly. "This bag has a mind of its own!" She pulled up the hood of her very yellow, very large rain jacket.

"Thanks for stopping it." I smiled wide to show her I was friendly, then narrowed the grin to "just pleasant" so she didn't think I wanted to hang out.

"So what are you doing, anyway? Recording on your phone? With a trash bag? In the middle of the rain? Right before a thunderstorm?" She looked at me through squinted eyes. "It's all kind of suspicious."

I took the wet bag she held out. "I have to clean up Mrs. Richardson's front step. There's a whole mess of toilet paper." I didn't feel like getting into the whole thing. "I'd better finish up before the storm."

"Wait," she said, as I turned back, "and this is important. Does the mess you're cleaning up involve clean toilet paper or used?" She walked next to me, uninvited.

I laughed despite myself. "Clean. Definitely clean."

"I was hoping so, since you're not in a hazmat suit, or wearing gloves. But I also don't know you at all, and maybe that's how you roll."

I laughed again. I could tell she was trying to be funny, and not trying to be mean.

"What's your name, anyway?"

Anyway. Like I was the new one in the neighborhood, not her. "Umm, I'm Sammy."

"Short for Samantha?"

"Samira."

"That's so pretty. I would have kept that name."

Kiera had shortened my name years ago, and I hadn't given it much thought since then.

"So, Sammy, why is there toilet paper on the ground? Who put it there? Was it you? Is that why you're cleaning up? Is this your house?" She shot off questions one after the other, reminding me what I didn't like about meeting new people.

I shoved toilet paper into the bags faster. "Mrs. Richardson lives here. She was TP'd yesterday and I'm helping clean up before the storm." She didn't need to know Mrs. Richardson had toilet papered her own house. Or that Kiera had toilet papered mine.

"This is not how houses get toilet papered where I come from." She held the bag open for me. I hadn't asked for her help, but I was happy for the assist.

I wondered where she moved from.

"We moved from downtown. Mom wanted me to go to school out here. Fresh start and all." She tied the handles of the bag closed. "Do you have more bags?"

I had underestimated the amount of paper and the weight added by the rain and the strength of the bags. I shook my head no. The rain was now a steady drizzle.

"We can get a few from Mrs. Richardson," she said, already ringing the doorbell before I could object. My morning was going from bad to worse.

"You moved here for a fresh start from what?" I asked, trying to shift the attention back to her.

Alice giggled, and nervously tugged at her hood. "Oh, you know. Everything."

15

Cookies with a Side of Cringe

"Oh my, the rain's coming down in sheets, isn't it?" Mrs. Richardson stood in the doorway, her usual spiky hair flat, her lips downturned. I side-glanced Alice to see if she got the pun. *Sheets* of toilet paper. She didn't react. Kiera would have gotten it. "You should come in from the lightning."

I hesitated. Thunder rumbled, and Alice jumped in the house, kicked off her wet shoes, and introduced herself before I had a chance to weigh the pros and cons of going inside: getting struck by lightning versus making polite conversation. I needed a minute. I stared at Alice's chipped pink toenail poking through her sock. I would have curled my toes under to hide the hole, but she didn't seem to care.

Mrs. Richardson's house was nothing like I expected.

She was always in black, from head to toe, like a bleak crayon, but her hallway was the most beautiful thing I had ever seen. Every bit of floor was covered in rugs of shaggy red, and soft blue, and rougher greens. The walls were painted in bright yellow and fluorescent pink swirls. There were mobiles of different shapes and colors hanging from the ceiling.

"Whoa," Alice said.

"Whoa?" Mrs. Richardson asked, her voice pinched with irritation.

This would be an amazing video for "My Home." If this was actually my home. Which it wasn't. If I had the courage to ask Mrs. Richardson to record. Which I didn't. I mentally flipped through my playlists to choose the right soundtrack for the video I wasn't going to make. This would have been Coldplay. Yes, definitely Coldplay.

Alice reached over her head and touched a bright red piece shaped like a lightning bolt. The mobile clinked.

"I need to get something from the oven," Mrs. Richardson said when a timer beeped in the kitchen. I wasn't imagining the smell of cookies after all. "You can wait in the living room if you'd like." She directed us with a tilt of her chin, her hands shoved into the pockets of her bathrobe.

"Are those cookies I smell?" Alice yelled behind her, into the kitchen. You don't invite yourself into a house and demand cookies. No matter how amazing they smelled. Alice was missing a politeness filter. "I could go for a couple." Or a filter of any kind.

"It's a little early for cookies, isn't it?" Mrs. Richardson asked, joining us in the living room.

Alice made herself comfortable on the couch, moving cushions to make space. I waited until Mrs. Richardson invited me to sit. She didn't.

"If it's not too early to make them, it's not too early to eat them," Alice replied. I cringed. Like really. My body actually jerked.

Her argument mobilized Mrs. Richardson back to the kitchen. "I guess that makes some sort of sense."

"What are you doing?" I asked under my breath. "Let's get going." I gestured to the door with both hands, to show her how quickly.

"What do you mean? There's pretty much a hurricane outside."

She was exaggerating. "It's barely even raining." A birdbath toppled over in the backyard on cue.

Mrs. Richardson came back with a plate of cookies for each of us. She still had not invited me to sit down and I shifted my weight to the other leg, pretending to look over the albums and thick glossy books that filled her bookshelf from floor to ceiling.

Alice fired off questions between bites. "Your name is on these paintings. Are you the artist? Were you famous? Is your stuff in a museum?"

I perched on the edge of an armchair, gripping my plate, not daring to eat a cookie, with its crumbly mess.

"Yes, I'm a painter," Mrs. Richardson said. Her face didn't soften, but her voice did. "Or I used to be."

I wondered why she didn't paint anymore, but Alice didn't give her a chance to answer the first questions before moving to the next. "What the heck happened on your front step?"

Mrs. Richardson adjusted her cardigan. "Oh, my house was toilet papered," she said, not making eye contact.

"Lady," Alice said. I doubted Mrs. Richardson had ever been spoken to that way. "I've seen toilet papering, and that's not how it's done."

Mrs. Richardson's eyes flickered to mine.

I spoke for her. "Mrs. Richardson laid the toilet paper on her own porch." I couldn't get myself to call it toilet papering. "She was trying to help out our family."

"Wait. What?" Alice's mouth stayed open, cookie crumbs sprinkling from the corners. Exactly as I had feared.

"Someone toilet papered our house yesterday." Was it only yesterday? "A for-real toilet papering. My brother was really upset that we were the only ones targeted. So Mrs. Richardson tried to toilet paper her own house."

"Umm, but you didn't want to do a better job?" Alice asked.

I knew the answer to this one too.

"She couldn't."

"That's true," Mrs. Richardson said. "Did your grandmother explain?"

The sky was still gray behind Mrs. Richardson, but the rain had stopped momentarily. "No, but it's pretty obvious."

"Obvious how?" Alice asked.

"I know Umma must have called you to toilet paper your own house. It sounds like a ridiculous ask, but I know you said yes." Both of them waited for me to go on. I shifted my weight, but stayed leaning on the arm of the chair. "Everything in your house is so neat; the books are lined up perfectly, the records are arranged alphabetically. You like things to be in order. You laid out the toilet paper in the same way." It was easier to speak if I didn't look at them. "But the top half of your bookshelf is dusty."

"So?" Alice asked.

"So, Mrs. Richardson wouldn't let dust collect on the top half of her shelves if she could help it." I could tell by the expression on her face that Alice still didn't understand. "Umma said you had to rest because you're having surgery. You didn't throw the toilet paper into the tree because you couldn't have."

"That's one hundred percent correct," Mrs. Richardson said. "I have shoulder surgery next month and I have to take care of my good shoulder as much as possible until I've recovered from that."

"Wow," Alice said. "Are you a genius or something?"

I didn't understand what the big deal was. All the signs were right there.

"Okay, Miss Smarty-Pants," Alice said, "so who toilet papered your house?"

"I don't know," I lied, because the only thing more embarrassing than telling someone your house was hit is admitting your ex–best friend was the hitter.

"But I know it wasn't Mrs. Richardson."

16

Back to School Already?

Once the rain slowed to a drizzle, I said quick good-byes before Alice had a chance to follow me out. She wouldn't care that I didn't ask her to. Invitations were optional to her.

I leaned against the door once I got home, missing Mom when I smelled her favorite peony-scented candles.

"Mrs. Richardson said you and new girl did good job cleaning up toilet paper," Umma said, walking around with her watering can. "How about some breakfast, molay?"

I had left the plate of cookies on Mrs. Richardson's kitchen counter untouched. "I could eat." Nothing mobilized Umma faster than someone being hungry.

I waited at the kitchen table, flipping through my phone. Exclamation points in different colors and sizes plastered the school's social media posts, across photos of yearbooks stacked on long white tables. The pictures were a little out of focus and blurry. Mrs. Markley was the first to admit she could teach us about picture depth and quality, but couldn't take a great photo herself. "Great at the theory, not great at the practical." That's what she said.

My phone froze on the last post and then turned off by itself. I really needed a new phone.

"Looks like the yearbooks came in and we're supposed to be at school tomorrow to help distribute them," I said, mouth already full with mangos Umma had placed in front of me in case I died from starvation before breakfast was ready.

"You want to go?" Umma asked. "I can call someone to drive you there. Your mom left some numbers."

"Olivia's mom is supposed to take me." I wasn't sure I was ready to return to school so soon. Not enough time had passed since the talent show, since the toilet papering. But I had spent all year working on the yearbooks, and I wanted to see them. The school was big enough that avoiding Kiera should have been easy.

I was wrong.

My Not-Home

I curled up in my beanbag with my laptop all evening, arranging and rearranging clips of videos. With the contest deadline less than two weeks away, I wanted Mrs. Markley to see what I was working on.

I had videos of Umma on her prayer mat with her forehead to the ground, Imran setting up entire towns of Lego people, our breakfast table of dosas, our pantry with containers of Kerala mixture and murukku and jars of homemade spicy pickles, our kitchen drawer dedicated to plastic bags from the grocery store, old yogurt containers washed and ready to store things, the TV playing Hindi movies and Malayalam news.

I added pictures of the toilet papered tree, deleted them, added them back, deleted them again.

The video didn't feel right, but I couldn't tell why. I

was hoping Mrs. Markley could. I tried adding clips of Zaara teaching Imran how to ride his bike and ones of all of us dressed up for Eid prayers.

Still, nothing made the video better.

I chose Yo-Yo Ma, then Taylor Swift, then Bollywood, then Mohammed Rafi.

Nothing made it feel like "My Home."

I closed the computer in frustration and went looking for Umma. My parents' curtains were closed. Their curtains were never closed. I passed Zaara's room and her bed was covered in a striped quilt, instead of the flowery one she had used for years.

My home didn't feel like home either.

No Is Not a Four-Letter Word

Toilet papering, cleaning Mrs. Richardson's front porch, getting to school early with the rest of yearbook club. Three days in a row I had been awake earlier than I should have been.

I had never hung out with Olivia outside of lunch and yearbook, but my guess was that she would be a morning person. She was bouncing up and down in the back seat. She was probably an any-time-of-day person. She chattered back and forth with her mom, filling all the talking space. I was grateful I didn't have to say much, but also missed having my own mom or dad there to drive me.

Olivia shot out of the car as soon as we pulled up to the school. "Come on, Sammy," she yelled over her shoulder, trying to get me to match her energy, her wildly waving arms begging me to hurry up.

The three white tables from Mrs. Markley's blurry social media posts were set up along the wall, under the basketball hoop that had been stuck midway up since the first day of school.

"They look amazing," Mrs. Markley said, moving books from one table to another. "Even better than I expected." Her bracelets clinked. "We have about fifteen minutes before it's nine o'clock, before the rest of the school gets here. I wanted you to have a little time with the books first."

The others from yearbook club were already there, flipping pages, admiring their work, remembering deadlines made and not made. Seeing my pictures bound in the yearbook made them feel real, but strangely unreal.

"My layouts and interviews look amazing," Olivia said. "So do your photos."

The gym squeaked with footsteps as the rest of seventh grade rushed in.

"Okay, people, take your stations," Mrs. Markley said, walking out from behind the table, ready to direct the crowds that were forming. "Once the books are distributed, you can join the signing party. Let me know if you need a break."

I stationed myself behind the last names from P to Z, as far as possible from the C table. At that point in the day I still believed I could somehow avoid Kiera Carter.

Friends stood in the wrong lines so they could be near each other, others who managed to separate themselves from their besties yelled across the room, a nerf football arced across the gym like a rainbow, drinks were spilled, quarters and dimes rolled everywhere when the cashbox was dropped not once, but twice. Finally, the last book was distributed. Olivia clutched her copy. "That was awesome! Now let's get them signed."

Kids lay on their stomachs or sat on the floor with their legs crossed, forming circles of different sizes with their yearbooks and markers in front of them. The yearbook club had split up, each of them finding their other group of friends. I didn't have another group of friends.

"Sammy," Mrs. Markley called out. "Your pictures look amazing, don't you think?"

I gave her a tiny nod and lingered at the table, unsure where to sit, what group to join.

"It would be great if we could get some pictures of the signing party." *Party* was a stretch of the word. Lemonade juice boxes and a few open containers of mini brownies were laid out in one corner of the gym, a few signs tacked to the wall directly above. Semi-festive signs because Mrs. Markley still didn't have colored ink in her printer.

"You know I'm useless at taking pictures," she said, holding the camera out for me. I grabbed the strap like a lifeline, not even pretending like I'd rather be huddling in circles with the others, signing books. "And come find me before you leave. I want to hear how you're doing with your videos for the contest."

I walked from group to group, relieved I didn't have to hover outside their little pods, hoping to find an opening next to someone I barely knew.

"Over here," someone yelled, waving an arm from across the room. "Take a picture of us." Her whole group grinned and pouted and duck-faced, even though my photos look so much better when no one is posing.

I circled a ring of friends, their heads bent over, almost touching in the middle. They made peace signs and bunny ears when they saw me with my camera.

"Hey, Sammy."

I didn't realize one of those heads was Kiera's until it was too late.

"Hi," I answered, happy Mrs. Markley's camera was big and clunky and able to hide most of my face. The rest of the talent show dance group was squeezed next to her.

"You're the one who backed out of the dance last minute, right?" the guy with the mustache asked. I couldn't tell if it was just a shadow or if he was actually growing a beard.

"Yeah." I lowered the camera a tiny bit. "That was me."

Kiera didn't look up from the book she was signing. "You never really explained why."

"I guess I woke up in the morning and wasn't feeling it." I pretended to zoom in on something through the lens, trying to walk away backward, stepping on someone's foot.

"And here I thought you changed your mind because your house got toilet papered. Bad omen and all that. My grandfather said they did quite the number on your tree."

I stepped over someone's outstretched legs, still trying to create distance between Kiera and me. "I wouldn't have known the moves or had the right costumes anyway." I was asking without asking.

Kiera looked up for a moment before bending over the yearbook in front of her again. "Oh yeah, you missed a couple rehearsals at the end. We changed a few things."

A few things? As in *every*thing.

"Wait, your house was toilet papered?" A girl with big hoop earrings popped her head up from a different circle.

I didn't want to talk about my tree being toilet papered, didn't need the whole room, the whole school to know. I stumbled over my words. "Yeah, on the last day of school." I circled the girls, clicking pictures like this conversation wasn't upsetting me, while my sweaty, shaky hands told a different story.

"Sammy always takes things so personally. It was probably just a prank," Kiera said. Mustache/beard boy chuckled and Kiera shoved him hard enough that he rolled back, still holding his knees.

Hoop-earring girl sat up, and the rest of her group followed her lead. "Last year someone left a pile of dog poop on our front step." She bit her upper lip. "They even arranged the bags like a pyramid so we would know it wasn't an accident. I didn't sleep for weeks."

I peeked over the camera. "Did you ever figure out who did it?"

She shook her head no, her earrings swaying.

I cleaned the camera lens, removing invisible smudges. "I guess waking up to the tree being toilet papered did make me feel sort of . . . weird."

"Weird is an understatement," Hoop-Earrings said. "I obsessed for months."

Kiera's voice was kinder to her than to me. "They were silly pranks. Not a big deal."

"Tell that to the person who's cleaning bags of dog poop off their front step," Hoop-Earrings said.

Or to the person whose front yard was toilet papered.

"Sammy, right?" Hoop-Earrings asked. I didn't think she knew my name. "A few of the girls are coming over to my house after this. You should come hang out."

I looked at her through the camera. It was a pity invite for sure, but I still had a hard time just saying no. "Olivia's my ride back home."

"Olivia is wild. We love her." She kneeled to see over the heads of everyone crouching and lying on their stomachs. "Hey, Olivia," she shouted across the gym. "Want to come hang out with us after yearbook signing?"

Like a prairie dog at the zoo, Olivia popped up on her knees from a different circle. "I can't. I'm leaving for my grandma's in Florida tomorrow morning. I have to go pack and have dinner with the family."

Hoop-Earrings tapped on her phone. "Let me check with my mom."

All those times I saw social media posts of people in our class together on the lake, at football games, getting ice cream, I had wished I was invited too. Now I finally was. And right in front of Kiera. So she could see I had people to hang out with too. I couldn't understand why a nervous ball at the pit of my stomach decided this was a good time to show up.

"All set. We can drop you back home," Hoop-Earrings said.

I had never said yes to the invitation.

I guess I had never said no either.

19

When You Don't Want What You Want

I dragged myself to the front of the school, hoping that if I walked slowly enough, time would turn back and I could say no to hanging out with girls I'd barely ever spoken to.

"You can do this, Sammy," I whispered to myself, repeating the words under my breath until they had no meaning. "It will be fun." I tried to convince myself even though I knew both statements were lies. I could not do this. It would not be fun.

I was alone at the front entrance, which made it easier to talk to myself, but harder to meet the girls I was supposed to be riding with. I didn't know their phone numbers or even their names.

A blue car drove around from the back of the school.

Hoop-Earrings was in the front seat. She and her mom smiled and waved. I waved back, relieved to see them although I didn't even want to go.

"You can do this, Sammy," I whispered to myself. "It will be fun," I said once more for good measure.

The car slowed down but didn't come to a complete stop. Kiera rolled down the back window. Kiera. "See you later, Sammy," she said, before turning to the girl next to her. "Turn up the music. I love this song." They drove away, the music drowning the chatter and laughter.

My phone buzzed with a text from an unknown number. Hey sorry you can't come to my house today. Kiera explained why you couldn't. Maybe next time. Hope you have a great summer!

I stood watching the back of the car, alone, which was what I had wanted, and confused, which was not what I had wanted. I felt like I had been toilet papered all over again.

Markley Magic

M rs. Markley was stacking chairs in the gym. "Sammy, you're still here. Great." She waved me closer with her free hand. "I was hoping we could talk about that contest."

"Umm, yeah." Let's pretend I stayed back for that, and not because I had been ditched at the front of the school recently enough that my face still felt hot. I hoped Mrs. Markley didn't notice.

I helped her roll stacks of chairs to the storage room behind the gym. I was happy to have something to occupy my hands and my thoughts. Mrs. Markley monologued about portaging at the Boundary Waters, her new kitten, about how my pictures looked so good in the yearbook. Like she knew I needed a moment to pull myself together. "I heard you getting some nice comments about your photos," she said, rearranging the tiny room to create space.

"People just like seeing pictures of themselves," I answered. I held the door open with my foot so she could pick up the rolls of construction paper that had fallen from a shelf.

"That's actually not true. Most people don't." She maneuvered the last stack of chairs one way and then the other to fit them in. "That's what makes your perspective special. You make people look like themselves."

I let her compliments replace the uneasiness that still prickled at my edges.

"Are you ready to talk about the contest?" She closed the door behind us and wiggled the knob. "Let's go to my room. I'm excited to hear your ideas."

I wasn't ready to share my video with anyone, but Mrs. Markley was the first one to see most of my work. I shook my phone three times. I don't know why three, but sometimes that helps get stuck videos unstuck. "I know it needs editing. Something doesn't feel right," I warned, before handing her my phone. I squirmed in my seat as she watched. The video felt babyish and my shots of spices and snacks felt too simple.

"It's fabulous," she gushed, but teachers had to say things like that. "I love the story you told about your home. But why don't you think it feels right?" She passed the phone back to me. "We can talk for hours about framing the shots differently or zooming in a little less, but none of that matters if you don't love what you have."

I pulled at my braid for comfort. "I feel like I'm looking at my house through someone else's eyes." I had included all the things I thought people would find interesting, all the Indian things, all the Muslim things. Things I often had to explain. "But I don't know if that's what I consider home."

She drummed her fingers on the table in thought. "Hmm . . . When I'm stuck, or something doesn't feel right, I like to take a break and come back with fresh eyes. Why don't you work on the second video, the one about community, and come back to this one?"

"I don't know what community really means," I admitted.

Mrs. Markley started packing up her things. "I would say yearbook is part of your community, your school, your teachers, your friends, your neighbors. Almost anything." We walked to her car talking about ideas, but also about movies and songs and her summer plans, and by the time she dropped me home and was introducing herself to Umma, I no longer had that terrible hot feeling in the pit of my stomach.

Pretty Sure Is Good Enough

The next morning I slept in until 10:46. Summer was finally going the way I had hoped. If I were in school, I'd be in pre-algebra now, struggling to find x.

I had a missed call from Zaara, and multiple texts from an unknown number.

hey I have a few ideas

about your toilet papering

mystery

Then a few minutes later—

I'm sure you want to figure it out right

"Figure it out, right?" like I was being given the option, or "figure it out right," like do it correctly?

No to both.

text me back

this is Alice

Why would she care so much about who toilet papered my house? The house wasn't hers. The neighborhood barely was.

I was pretty sure who had toilet papered my house. Pretty sure was good enough for me.

The Who of Whodunit

The house was in full swing downstairs. Blankets with polka dots and stripes and dinosaur prints were propped up by chairs and tables forming a central hub with tunnels extending like spider legs. I recorded Umma crawling out of one.

"Oof, Imran, these knees are too old for magic tunnels. Me being able to stand up again is magic enough," Umma said, her hands on her knees, taking a moment to straighten out before untucking the pallu of her saree from her waist. "Oh, you're awake, Sammy. We were missing you."

There were no accusations for wasting most of the morning. I missed Mom, but didn't miss her "seize the day" vibes.

"Umma, did you give our new neighbor my phone

number?" Her look of guilt made me immediately sorry for my tone.

"I did. Alice came here three times already, so I gave her your number. I know you like text better. I was wrong?"

Oh, big-time wrong.

"No, you're right, Umma. I prefer texts." That part was true. The universe had told me loud and clear that I didn't need new friends. I could be one of those famous movie directors who never left their homes. Mysterious, intriguing, a recluse.

Imran emerged from another tunnel. "I like Alice." Imran liked everyone, and thought everyone liked him. I wish he were right. "She wants to help get to the bottom of the great toilet paper caper." He grabbed a few Lego blocks and disappeared into the maze again.

There was no caper. "You still want to figure that out?" I asked. I thought the Richardson bait and switch had worked.

He popped his head through a spot where two blankets were held together with a binder clip. "Not help me, silly. Help *you*."

I clipped the blanket shut for him again. "I don't care who did it," I answered. "Maybe I don't want to know."

"That's not what Zaara said." Like a whack-a-mole, his

head popped out from a different spot.

"You spoke to Zaara?" I asked, while Umma plated a crispy dosa for me, swaying her hips to the song she was humming.

"Yeah, but they were going to bed, so you'll have to wait until tonight to call them." The time difference was so confusing. Mom was right. Sleeping in and staying in my room had made me miss out.

"Crispy dosa, Sammy. You love this."

I did. I tore off a piece to dunk in the small bowl of steaming sambar.

"I think I already know who toilet papered the house," I said quietly to Umma.

She waited, spatula in hand, for me to say more. I swirled another piece of dosa in the sambar, not looking up. "I think it was Kiera," I mumbled, eyes down, mouth full.

Umma leaned in, spatula near her ear to somehow help her hear better. "Who, molay?"

I swallowed but didn't look up. "Kiera," I mumbled through my dosa, barely audible.

She cupped my chin, lifting my face toward hers. "Your friend? Why would she do such thing?" I shrugged. "Like joke? Prank you play on each other?" Her grip kept my chin in place so I had no choice but to use my words.

"No, I don't think she meant it to be . . . fun." Or funny.

She let go of my face and paused. Umma is not a pauser. Her wrinkles deepened. "You are sure?"

I've known Kiera forever. It was her. I nodded yes.

"She told you?" I shook my head no.

"You saw her do it?" I shook my head no.

"Someone else saw her?" I shook my head no.

"I just know, Umma."

She stepped back to the stove and spread another dosa, pursing her lips in thought. "Sometimes, Sammy, guessing is not enough."

It felt like enough.

"You decide, Sammy. Thinking someone did like that"—she pointed to the tree with her spatula—"is big deal. What's word? Accuse? It is important to be sure." Her wrinkles softened, as did her tone. "How little girl even reach so high? Pete says he never saw like that."

"I don't know how she did it, and I'm not sure why. But I know it was her." The dosa caught in the middle of my chest and I took a sip of water.

Imran popped up from his fort. "Know what? know who?" I trusted Umma to not tell Imran, to not tell anyone.

Umma rubbed an onion on the pan. "When I was little,

my sister and I share a room. Our favorite lamp was broken. I don't care one bit. But my sister, she couldn't stop until she knows who broke lamp. She wasted so much time asking everyone."

Part of Imran's dome collapsed behind him. "Who broke the lamp, Umma? Did she ever find out?"

Umma was back to swaying and humming. She stopped to look at me, eyes wide open, mischievous smile. "I never told a single person before." She slid another dosa on my plate, squeezing it next to the one I had barely touched. "It was me. I broke the lamp." And she burst into her wild, loud cackle. Imran couldn't help but join. Neither could I.

I'm the Worry?

Three more texts from Alice before I gave up hope of ignoring her.

Sure, I texted back, even though she hadn't asked a question to which "sure" would have been an appropriate answer. At least Alice hadn't witnessed me being ditched in front of the school the day before. For all she knew I was totally socially savvy, the kind of person who had so many friends that when someone named Michelle invited me to a party on Friday I would have to ask which Michelle and which Friday.

Be there in three minutes, she texted back immediately.

I didn't have time to figure out what I had agreed to before the bell rang, definitely *less* than three minutes later. Her skateboard was covered in stickers of monkeys and pandas, but also tiaras and big bubble letters of words like *Harpoon*, and others that made no sense, like *Flong*. She wore black jeans that hung low, a flannel tied around her waist, and a beanie pulled back so far I wasn't sure how the cap was staying on her head.

"Whoa! It's already hot out there," she said, letting herself in. Umm, maybe don't wear flannel and a beanie in summer? She opened the right cabinet to help herself to a glass of water. In her world, four visits must have been enough to make herself feel at home. In my world it was forty.

"You know what's great when it's hot. Nice, cold lassi," Umma said.

I had barely put away my plate after breakfast.

"Hey, Alice," Imran said from somewhere within the blanket maze.

"Hey, Ronny." Which made Imran snort with laughter. She had a nickname for him already? How long had I been sleeping?

"I've got so many ideas about how we can do this." She lifted her notebook and pencil for me to see. "I brought supplies."

Had I agreed to all of this with my one-word text? "Do what?" I asked.

"Solve the mystery of who TP'd your tree! Don't you want to?" Her eyebrows knitted into disbelief, her beanie barely hanging on.

"I guess I haven't thought about it much." Not true at all. My phone rang with a photo of Zaara and me squeezed into one sleeping bag.

"Zaara!" I was a little embarrassed to be talking to her in front of a stranger. Even if this stranger knew where we kept our water glasses and had a nickname for my younger brother. "Imran said you'd be asleep." She had never been in a different country from me, separated by oceans and continents.

"I thought I'd try once more before we went to bed. Looks like you're living it up without Mom and Dad around. What time is it there?"

"It's almost eleven thirty."

"And you're still in pj's? Wow!"

I wanted to reach across the screen and touch her. "How're things there? Is it weird to be in India without Umma?" I asked.

"For sure. The Wi-Fi is slow. So we might get disconnected." Umma would have fixed that in a moment with her secret weapon. "Any updates on the toilet papering?"

Alice popped up behind me on my screen. "Hey, I'm Alice, your new neighbor." She waved. "We were about to start figuring that out." Next-level annoying.

"Hey, Alice." Zaara waved back. I took the phone to the office for privacy. "Mom and Dad feel terrible about leaving you there with the toilet papered house. That's all they can talk about." The frame froze for a minute and her voice caught up. "They worried even more because they thought you were hiding in your room this morning when we called." She lowered her voice even though there wasn't anyone else in her room. "They were even talking about cutting the trip short."

"They're thinking of cutting their trip short because of me?" I asked. That was Imran's role, not mine. "I'm going to be in my room a lot over the next two weeks, but there's a reason." I told Zaara about the contest and the videos I was editing. "Besides, everything is totally under control here. We're investigating the toilet papering," I lied. "Alice even brought supplies."

"Oh, Mom and Dad will be thrilled. And relieved."

I shook the phone three times and it unstuck. "What about you? Are you having a good time?" I asked.

Zaara tucked her hair behind one ear, the way she did when she was nervous. "I guess. But I miss you guys." She tucked her hair behind the other ear; this double-tuck was new. "There's so much going on here. They want me to be in one of the dances for the wedding, and they've been practicing for weeks already. We have to go shopping for clothes. There's a party scheduled every evening. I wish you were here."

Zaara was nervous about parties and people? That

was my role, not hers.

"When do you get to visit the school? Hand over the check?" I asked.

She smiled and let go of her hair. "Tomorrow. I'm so excited. I've seen all their pictures and I know so many names, but I can't wait to meet them in real life."

She tilted her head and smiled at me. "See what you did there? You made me feel better right away. You always do. Just like Umma, she and you—"

"Zaara," I yelled into the screen. "Zaara." No amount of shaking woke up my phone.

Alice was waiting for me right outside the office door. I had known she would be.

"Let me get dressed," I told her. "And then we can get to work." Working together to solve a mystery wasn't ideal. Especially when I already knew the answer. Even if I missed my family, I didn't want them to cut their trip short because of me.

"Excellent," Alice said. "What about you, Imran? You can help too."

His voice came from somewhere deep inside the blanket fort. "Nah, I don't want to."

Me neither.

24

Ninja Rolls of Toilet Paper

Alice followed me. Up the stairs. Where I was going to get dressed. I knew it was best to say something right away, if only I could make myself.

Dad baked black forest cake for my eighth birthday after I saw it in a magazine and begged him. He spent so much time decorating with cherries and little icing unicorns, and I ended up hating how it tasted but couldn't get myself to tell him. Now I got black forest cake every year.

"I'll get dressed and meet you downstairs if that's okay." I drew a very small border of what I wanted around me, a tiny line in the ground.

"Sure," she said, turning back around.

That wasn't bad. No hurt feelings, and now I'm not stuck with a lifetime of black forest friendship.

By the time I returned, Alice and Imran were giggling in the center of the blanket fort. Now that Zaara was gone, I was the one who was supposed to be in the middle of his forts.

"I'm ready to get started, Alice." Enough with the giggling.

The fort quivered and the blanket pulled away from the top of the chair, collapsing the whole structure. "Whoops. My bad, Imran," she said. "I can help you put the blankets back up before we go."

My eyes darted to Imran. Someone who had known my brother for more than a minute would be careful inside one of his creations. Soggy Marie biscuits and unsteady blanket forts could send Imran spiraling. He stood in the middle of the destruction, dusting himself off. "I was kind of done with the fort anyway."

Alice high-stepped out of the center of the mess she had created. "Need help cleaning up?"

"Not really. I'm the best at putting away blankets." He sifted through the pile, looking for the right one. He liked to fold by age of blanket, and then by color.

"All right, buddy, see you soon." She held her hand out for Imran to high-five. Buddy? Was she someone's coach? She'd better not try to "buddy" me. I'd have to draw another line.

"I thought we could start by investigating the scene of the crime," she said.

So dramatic.

I followed her outside, watching while she walked around the tree—stepping back and to the side, looking up the tree and down the street, tapping her forehead with the pencil eraser the entire time. When she circled the tree for the third time, I stepped in.

"What are you looking for, anyway?"

"Clues." She flipped over one of the stones at the base of the tree.

"And did you find any?"

"Little ones." She tried to wrap her arms around the trunk, hugging or measuring.

"Like what?"

"Like why there are no footprints around the trunk." She rubbed a pinch of dirt between her fingers as if she knew what she was looking for.

"Well, it's mostly grass around the tree, so you wouldn't see any footprints, and the rain would have wiped everything away," I explained, not at all impressed with her investigative skills. "And if someone was coming to toilet paper the house, they wouldn't stand so close to the trunk. Actually, they'd have to stand way back, probably on the road." I pictured Kiera, in the dead of night, dressed head to toe in black, ninja rolling and hurling toilet paper. Except Kiera could never even throw a water balloon across her grandparents' pool.

"I wonder how they got the toilet paper all the way to the top of the tree. You'd need to be pretty strong to make that happen," I said.

"Go on." Alice scribbled in her notebook, finally using her pencil as more than a forehead tapper.

"Plus, you didn't see the tree that morning. It was completely covered, every side. Totally symmetric."

"Okay . . ."

I stepped away from the tree and threw an invisible roll of toilet paper. "Someone with a good arm, a really good arm, could stand far back enough on the road to hit the top."

"Yes?"

I walked to the side near the house. "But there's not enough space on this side to stand back and throw."

"So that means . . ."

"So that means they needed some sort of launcher to shoot the toilet paper up there." I held my hands together, pointing my arm-launcher to the top of the tree. "Like a water gun, but for toilet paper."

Alice was scribbling madly in her book. "Wow. You figured all that out? Like right now?"

All I had done was look around and notice things. "I bet you would have noticed, too, if you had seen the tree. I have a bunch of pictures I took that morning. I can show you later." I hadn't downloaded any TP pictures to my phone—I didn't want them on there, and had decided not to include them in any of my three videos. They didn't belong in my home, or community, or even the world.

"We should write this all down while it's fresh. It gets confusing later."

That seemed like a lot of work. "Why do you care so much?" I asked. I didn't mean to sound rude. Alice was new, she didn't know any of us, and she hadn't even seen the toilet paper. The question was valid.

"I don't know."

I bet she did. Almost every time I say I don't know, I do. So, I gave her a moment.

"Well, I guess I really do," she said.

I sat on the porch step, the bricks rough on the back of my legs.

"Maybe if I had asked more questions, if I proved the truth, we wouldn't have had to move."

I hoped this was one of those times Alice kept talking when she wasn't asked.

25

Period.

"The other day at Mrs. Richardson's, you asked me why I needed a fresh start," Alice said, sitting next to me on the step. "My last year was pretty messed up." That was something we had in common. I wondered if her house was toilet papered by the best friend who dumped her.

A wasp buzzed around us, but I kept my seat, willing it to move on. Alice didn't budge. "You're not going to tell anyone, right?"

I shook my head. Who'd I tell anyway? Maybe Zaara. Maybe Umma. "You mean, like, friends from school?"

"Yeah."

Well, that was easy enough. I didn't have any.

"Last year I was run out of school," Alice said. I imagined mobs with pitchforks. "Okay," she continued, "I know I can be a little dramatic. I didn't get run out." I erased the pitchforked mobs. "But I embarrassed myself so badly I had no choice."

Based on that criteria, I would not have made it past first grade.

"I mean, like, really badly." Okay, maybe third grade.

"I don't know if you're on social media much, but I'm a pretty big deal online." She turned her face to me, to see if I recognized her. I shook my head no. "I do makeup and hair tutorials."

"Sooooooo," she started slowly, "there was a new girl at school. You know how hard it can be to make friends." Even when you weren't a new girl. "Halfway through the year, I hadn't seen her at a single school event, and she was still eating lunch by herself." Thank you to the yearbook club for saving me from that fate. "But the worst possible thing happened to her." The skateboard slid down the wall and clattered near our feet. "We were in science class and she was wearing this great outfit. I told her I loved her white skirt." I had a feeling I knew where this story was going. "She stood up to write something on the board, and . . ."

"No," I said, covering my mouth with my hands.

"Yes," Alice replied. "Devastating. I would have jumped up and given her my sweater or a jacket, but I had nothing with me."

"She got her period right in front of the class?" I asked.

It was my worst fear. Okay, one of my many worst fears.

Alice nodded. "Once she understood the laughter and comments, she ran out of class and we didn't see her for the rest of the day."

I covered my face with my hands like I was that girl.

"I decided to make her my friend, hang out with her, walk with her to classes. I know. I'm a saint." I wasn't sure if she was trying to be funny or not. Alice picked at the light pink scab through the hole in her jeans, even though it wasn't ready to come off. "I tried waving to her in the hallway, but she ran away. At lunch I tried to invite her to my table, but she avoided me."

She worked her fingernail under the border of the scab, making her way to the middle.

"I came up with this brilliant idea. I have thousands of followers, and a lot of them go to our school. I went on this rant. Believe it or not, I can rant."

I had no trouble believing it.

"I ranted about being nice to each other, about what happened to the girl at school, about periods being natural and not something we should be embarrassed about." She nodded as she spoke, like she was approving herself. "And then I did what my social studies teacher had taught us. I called everyone to action." She paused for effect.

She was more than a little dramatic.

"I asked everyone to wear a red stain the next day." She leaned to one side and patted her butt to show me where. "On their pants, shorts, skirt, whatever. In solidarity." She pumped her fist in the air. "I'll be honest. I was a little nervous the next day. What if I was the only one in school with a big red mark on the back of my pants?"

She finally pulled off the last bit of the scab, holding it up proudly. Settle down, I wanted to tell her, it's a scab, not a bear you wrestled to the ground. She flicked it away.

"I didn't have to worry. Everyone came through. The school was a sea of white with red circles. Like, period." She put both her hands in front of me, shaping them into a circle. "Get it? Period? But also PERIOD." She could get a pun after all.

"I looked for the girl at lunch, in the halls, at science class where this whole thing started. I really hoped she felt all the support we were showing her."

Her scab showed a tiny dot of blood.

"Then I was called to the principal's office," she said. "I'm not going to lie. I thought she was calling to thank me, to tell me what a good job I was doing, sticking up for every woman. Ending bullying with a single video post." She pumped her hand in the air again, but brought it back down. "I was so wrong. Apparently the girl saw all of us in our red stains and thought the whole school was bullying her. I was suspended for three days."

She used her thumb to wipe away the spot of blood.

"Whoa," I said. "But didn't they see your video?"

"My mom made sure they watched it. But it didn't make a difference. They kept saying the words 'zero tolerance policy,' and that telling her story without her permission was unkind. They were convinced I was making fun of her, mocking her. And that's not even the worst part."

"It's not?"

"When I got back to school, I wanted to apologize to her and set the facts straight. In the three days I was gone, everyone started to believe I really was the bully. That I had convinced them to be bullies too. They had lessons in class and speakers came to talk to us about how our words and actions can be powerful."

"Wow."

"Yeah, wow. I know words can be powerful. I know actions can be powerful. That's how I was trying to help."

I thought about the girl coming to school and seeing everyone in their white clothes and red periods. Of course she thought the whole school was in on the plan.

Girls like her. Girls like me. We didn't assume people were trying to lift us up.

"I couldn't convince anyone otherwise. We had to leave."

"And your mom let you? Mine would never." Mom would have made me stay and face the consequences.

Alice stood up with a hop and a big smile, but I could see tears in her eyes. "We would have probably moved soon anyway. This time was for me, not for Mom. And now I've learned that I can't jump in to fix everything. But I still want to help others fix things for themselves."

She put both her hands on her hips and looked off in the distance. "I'm a superhero, stopping injustices everywhere before they ruin people's lives." She joked to cover the hurt.

I recognized the trick.

Push-Ups and Pull Downs

I had been expecting a Kiera-free summer.

Banking on it. Hoping for it.

Wrong again.

Alice and I were in my front yard the next day. She had been transformed from skater to anime girl, with a bright pink wig of pigtails cascading to her waist, a pink plastic shirt, and bright green silk pants with boots that zipped to her knees. She wore a striped tie to complete the outfit, and headphones hung around her neck. I'm pretty sure they weren't connected to anything.

"Come on, Sammy, we have clues to hunt. The clock is ticking," she said. I had no idea how or where she expected to go hunting. Or what the clock was counting down to. "How much longer until they get here?"

I checked my phone like I had two minutes ago when

she last asked. "They haven't texted." We were waiting for the person Mom had hired to install a video door-bell, so they could see everyone who came and went, with or without rolls of toilet paper in their arms.

We sat, leaning against the tree. Alice talked about everything and nothing, which got me to do the same. She told me she was scared of the dark. I told her I believed in aliens but not ghosts. She told me her mom moved whenever she got antsy and she had been through five schools already. I told her how Mom made me join every different club she could find. She told me how she started her makeup tutorials. I told her about the videos I was working on for the contest, and without worrying about what she would think or say, I showed her clips of what I was putting together for "My Community."

"Wow," Alice said, her shirt squeaking as she leaned around the tree to hand my phone back. "That's amazing! You're basically a professional! I bet you'll win."

"I don't think so," I said, but I didn't mind the idea. "But everywhere I look, I wonder if something would be part of my community, or part of my home."

"I'm the same way about color combinations for my videos. Like the purple of that flower next to the green of the grass. That would probably make a great outfit for a tutorial," she said. "I can't wait to see your next videos!"

I cupped my hand over my eyes like a visor to see who was coming down the street. Kiera was pulling a wagon behind her. My house was on one side of a U, and Kiera's grandparents' was on the other. We walked the short way when ice cream was melting and the long way when we wanted our swimsuits to dry. Kiera was walking the long way, talking to Mustache-Boy. He flipped his hair one way and then the other. Her giggle was high-pitched and fake.

Shielded by the tree, Alice had no idea what was coming our way. I wished I could keep them separated forever.

"Hey, Sammy," Kiera said. "I brought back the stuff I borrowed for the talent show." Alice ignored my silent messages for her to stay where she was, her clothes crinkling as she stood.

"Hey," Alice said, leaning across me to see Kiera, one of her pink pigtails tickling my nose. I moved the hair aside.

"Wait . . ." Kiera was taken by surprise. She looked Alice up and down, and she must have passed some test I never would, because Kiera introduced herself. "I'm Kiera. This is David." Mustache-Boy had a name.

"Alice," she replied, pointing at herself with both index fingers curled toward her.

"Cool outfit," Kiera said. She lifted the handle of the Radio Flyer for me to take, so I knew I was still there.

"Thanks. My mom's a personal shopper. People pay her, and she travels all over the place finding clothes for them." All the different looks was her favorite part of her mom's job. "I get a bunch of freebies I can then put together."

Kiera looked impressed.

Like me, David didn't have much to say. Maybe he was the quiet type too. He fell to the ground and started doing push-ups. "Got to strength train any chance I get. Coach's orders." Which, of course, made things even stranger.

"My grandparents have a pool. You should come swim," Kiera said, leaning into Alice. "You have an eyelash." She pressed her finger on Alice's cheek before offering it to her. Who touches someone's face as soon as they meet? "Make a wish."

David counted out his push-ups under his breath. "Eight, nine."

I felt like an intruder in my own yard. "Umm, I'm supposed to check the mousetraps in the basement today." Both of them looked at me with faces scrunched in disgust. "I mean, that would be my wish, I guess. That there's no mouse in the trap." I know exactly how to pull a conversation down, make things weird. David's push-ups. My pull downs.

They went back to their conversation. "Wow," Kiera said. "How'd you do that thing around your eye? I can never get that right."

I hadn't been sure about Alice's outfits until Kiera confirmed they were cool, but even I could tell her makeup and green upper eyelids would be popular.

"I can show you. I have a YouTube channel all about cosmetics and thrifting." She scrolled through her phone to show Kiera.

"Wait, I thought I recognized you," Kiera said. "I *love* your videos."

"Eighteen. Nineteen," David kept counting. I'm pretty sure he skipped over a few numbers.

"Wow, that outfit is amazing," Kiera said, zooming into a photo on Alice's phone. I craned my neck to see and she tilted her hand just enough so I couldn't. Subtle, but I noticed. "I can't wait to see your closet. It must be incredible!"

Alice slid her phone back into her pocket. "I haven't had a chance to unpack. Sammy and I have been pretty busy."

Kiera ignored the mention of me. "So what do you think about going swimming?"

"Want to go, Sammy? After they fix your doorbell?" Alice asked.

David added grunting to his counting. "Twenty-eight." Grunt. "Twenty-nine." Grunt. Yup, he was definitely skipping numbers.

"Umm, maybe next time," I said. "I've got some stuff I have to do first." I had no stuff. I knew it. Kiera knew it.

"Of course, Sammy. The mice," she said with a smirk.

"Yeah, we'll come next time," Alice said. "I'll unpack all the rest of my makeup and we can do these eyes." She batted her lashes, long and curved with a hint of pink in them, at Kiera.

I pulled the wagon into the garage, and David finally stood up. "Fifty," he said. He didn't even do twenty, I thought.

"Go ahead, Alice. Umma needed my help with something, so I'll be busy anyway."

She turned her back to Kiera and wiggled her eyebrows at me like we were in on a secret. "You sure? What about the investigation?"

"Oh, Sammy's fine. She's never liked swimming much. Come on, David." Kiera walked away, pulling Alice by her arm.

My chest squeezed as I watched them leave together. I hated myself for being jealous, but I couldn't help it.

I didn't want a friend for the summer anyway.

I squinted my eyes until they were blurry and hid behind the camera and recorded them as they walked away. To put distance between us. So I could pretend the scene was a movie I wasn't part of.

Shy and Quiet

I sat in my room not wanting to watch the shows, or listen to the playlists, or edit the videos that seemed exciting a few days ago. Kiera and Alice were probably already doing cannonballs into the pool. Alice, with her wild outfits, million followers, and green eye shadow, was more likely to be Kiera's friend than mine.

I dialed Mom's number.

"Hello?" Her voice was slurred. "Sammy, okay there?" she asked, her sentences jumbled from being pulled out of a dream.

"Whoops, sorry, Mom, everything is fine. I didn't mean to wake you." I hung up quickly, having miscalculated the time difference.

Zaara called back and I realized how much I missed them when I heard her voice. "I am so sorry, Zaara. I got the time all wrong and woke you guys up." Even though my fifth grade teacher told me I "should" be good at math and science because I was Indian, I was not. "You know I get mixed up when I subtract sometimes. Is it like five a.m.?"

Zaara's voice was fully awake. Her hair was probably done too. "I was up anyway."

"I loved the photos you sent." There were pictures of her handing over the check at the school, kids on her lap, one on her shoulders, the rest squeezed in next to her.

"I had an amazing time with them. Worth every single T-shirt sale." My phone buzzed and I accepted her request to switch to a video call. I was right. She looked perfect. "They're going to use the money I raised to build a new playground—built specifically for kids on the spectrum. They're so excited."

The sun hadn't even come up on that side of the globe, but Zaara was already changing the world.

"What about you, Sammy? Alice seems nice." The mirror behind Zaara was covered in Post-its of every size and color.

"Yeah, she's okay. I think she may be more a Kiera-type person than a Sammy type, though." I tilted my phone so she could only see my nose and mouth, in case my eyes got watery. *I* knew I didn't want to make new friends over summer, but my tear ducts didn't always understand.

"What does that even mean?" Zaara asked. "I'd kill to be your friend." Of course she had to say that. She's my sister.

"I think she's too, umm, cool to be friends with me. She's into makeup and clothes and all that stuff. She has more in common with Kiera. I'm probably too quiet and shy for her."

Zaara turned on a light so her face wasn't covered in shadows. "You say quiet and shy like it's a bad thing. I like quiet and shy." She'd be the only one. "You're such a good listener, and that makes for a good friend. You're fun to hang out with because you're funny and you notice things other people don't." She moved the phone even closer to her face. "Besides, makeup and hair is outside stuff. Do you like Alice's inside stuff?"

I kind of did. She was loud and pushy, but she was also nice and never made me feel like I was boring or ridiculous.

"Yeah, I guess."

"Well, that's what matters, right? I liked her energy on the phone the other day. And you know I never liked Kiera."

It was true. Zaara thought Kiera was phony.

"I never liked the way she talked to you, and I never liked how you let her talk *for* you. You're better off without her, Sammy."

"Zaara," I said, drawing out her name, but then smushing my words together so I wouldn't back out. "I think Kiera is the one who toilet papered the house." She had warned me about Kiera so many times. She could have said "I told you so," and she would have been so right. If the roles were reversed, I might have taken the opportunity.

"Oh, Sammy," she said, her voice full of pity, "I'm so sorry."

I would have felt better if she said "I told you so."

"That must have made the toilet papering a million times worse for you, worse than if a stranger did it."

She was right. "Can we talk about something else?" I asked. "Please."

She hesitated, furrowing her brow. "I guess, if that's what you want." She pulled a few Post-its off her mirror, bringing a blue one close to the camera for me to see. "I bet you can't guess what all these are. Dance moves. I know. Silly." I knew she was trying to sound upbeat for me. "Everyone's been rehearsing for weeks and I have no idea what I'm doing, so I wake up early to practice."

She treated dance practice like a school project. Hard work and Post-its.

"I'm so glad I don't have to be in the dance," I said, watching her study the note, moving one arm over her head.

She pulled two more off the mirror and studied them. "I wish I didn't either."

"Why don't you tell them?" Easier said than done. I should know.

"Everyone would be so disappointed. And I kind of want to . . . fit in." I never thought of Zaara as someone who had to work to fit in. "One of the girls already teases me because apparently I say my name wrong."

"That's ridiculous. You can say your name any way you want to."

"I know." She rolled her eyes. "I would back out, but Mom and Dad like the idea of me participating." She tucked her hair behind her ear and chewed her lower lip.

"You go ahead, Zaara. Get some practice. I can talk to you later. Love you, Zee."

I was usually the one being forced to participate. I understood exactly how Zaara must have been feeling.

Basket-Riding, TP-Cleaning Pete and His Band

I went looking for Umma and Imran, finding a note on the kitchen counter instead.

"Gone to Dana's. There's gulab jamun in frij if hungry."

Like a chipmunk, I filled each cheek with a GJ, too impatient for the microwave even though I preferred them warm. With five of us coming and going, and Zaara's T-shirt customers ringing the doorbell constantly, and Imran's autism therapists rotating through, I wasn't used to a quiet house. I reached for the comfort of my camera. I crouched eye-level with Imran's town of Lego figures, and followed their gaze under the sofa, where another town of Lego people looked back at me. I laughed out loud, and the sound echoed eerily. I popped two more gulab jamuns in my mouth before heading to

Mrs. Richardson's.

I corner-eyed Alice's house on the way, wondering whether she was inside or still swimming. Kiera's grandparents had a slide and a diving board. We had spent hours perfecting the timing of her dive and my slide to make one flawless splash. I wondered if they were doing the same.

Mrs. Richardson's garage door was open, and I could hear the famous Pete and his band. The idea of walking, uninvited, into the garage where the band was playing made my heart pound and my palms sweat. Umma was wrong. They weren't good at all. Their music was a chaotic mess of notes. I took a couple steps back, hoping they wouldn't look up from their instruments and see me lurking. Imran came bounding from the house into the attached garage, jumping down the stairs, cape flying.

His mouth moved in the shape of my name, but I couldn't hear over the noise.

"Sammy," he tried again, waving with both hands.

I took another step back, wondering if I could go back home without drawing attention to myself.

"Pete said I could sing the next song. You've got to watch." I didn't have to ask what song, but he told me anyway. "'Starfish and Coffee.' You know the words.

You should sing too. But backup. I'm the main singer." He dragged me by the hand, toward the house. "That's Pete," Imran said.

I hadn't expected Umma's friend to have a bald head covered in tattoos, or an earring with a hole so big I could see right through his lobe. His eyes were closed and his grin was wide as he plucked his guitar. If I focused on only him, I could hear music, not noise. He probably closed his eyes to do the same.

"Come on," Imran said, as he sat down cross-legged on the driveway. "Umma and Mrs. Richardson are making tea, but they'll come out to watch my song. They promised."

I let him pull me down to sit next to him.

The band was weirdly mismatched. The guy on the keyboard, the one Umma said was amazing, wore a purple Vikings ball cap, and his T-shirt had the Teenage Mutant Ninja Turtles on the front with "Acapulco" written underneath. Were these Turtles from Mexico? His mouth was turned to one side with his tongue sticking out as he concentrated. His stubble and clothes made him look like the dads in our school pick-up line. His hands flew over the keys so fast I couldn't see where they landed. When I focused on only what he was playing, the tune was beautiful, like a waterfall or swimming in the lake.

"I'm so excited," Imran said. "I wish I knew where my Prince costume was."

The drummer was a woman with skin a little lighter than mine, a big studded nose ring, and curly hair that took up the entire room. My hand smoothed my single tight braid. Her drumbeat was solid. You could tell she was the kind of person who didn't step away backward when a garage door was open with a band practicing inside.

I had never been part of an audience that was smaller than the band, and I felt exposed. I was glad Umma and Mrs. Richardson would be there when Imran started his song so I wouldn't be an audience of one.

"You guys, this is my sister Sammy," Imran said when the sound wound down.

"Hey, Sammy," they said back, and the drummer waved with her sticks.

If ever there was a time for a magical hole to appear and suck me down, this would be it.

"You ready, Imran?" they asked.

"Oh yeah, I was born ready." He really had been.

Umma and Mrs. Richardson joined us, holding glasses of iced tea and laughing like old friends. Umma had only been in the country for ten days.

"Perfect timing!" Imran squealed. "I'm about to start."

Cool Drummer, as she would forever be called in my head, pulled her sticks out of her hair, where she had left them. "You ladies want to do backup?"

"Backup what?" Umma asked.

"Singers, dancers, whatever you want," Cool Drummer explained.

They giggled like kindergarteners. "Let's do it."

"What about you?" Cool Drummer asked, pointing at me with her drumsticks.

I could stand in front of them by myself or I could be a backup singer.

See, this was why I should never leave my room. The choices were never great.

The Wrong Side of the Camera

"Umm, I guess I'll do backup," I said.

Umma gave me a one-armed hug, iced tea in her other hand. Mrs. Richardson nodded in my general direction. The three of us filled the gap between the keyboard and drums, Imran directly in front of us.

Of course I knew the song. You couldn't live in our house and not. Imran had a different passion of the moment every couple months, and one year after watching Prince perform on Sesame Street, that was the only music we were allowed to play. Imran liked the tune right away but became obsessed with the lyrics when Mom told him there were rumors that the song was about a girl who may have been on the autism spectrum.

If Imran had a theme song, this would be it.

If I had a theme song, it would be the instrumental

music you heard in the orthodontist's office. You vaguely recognized the tune but waited for the chorus to be sure.

They played the introduction and Imran started singing right on cue. At first, he held his arms stiff by his sides, with his hands balled into fists; his voice was too loud and then too soft. Umma and Mrs. Richardson immediately started with "ooooh-la-las" as if they had practiced. I was the only one who didn't know what was going on.

I half-heartedly mumbled a few "ooh-la-las" before giving up and trying to follow their moves. Umma would start a hip sway, Mrs. Richardson would follow, and then I would do the same or risk being the odd one out. Then Mrs. Richardson would start a finger snap, Umma next, and finally I would follow.

Imran's singing was terrible, but his arms loosened up, and the microphone stopped screeching. "This is what she'd say . . ." Imran sang pointing to us with the microphone. Umma and Mrs. Richardson looked at each other confused. I was the only one who knew the words.

"Starfish and coffee," I almost whispered.

Mrs. Richardson and Umma echoed my words.

"Maple syrup and jam."

They echoed again.

It's impossible to sing that song and be quiet or sad or unsure of yourself, but I was glad when the chorus was done and Imran took over again.

I couldn't concentrate on Imran or the music or the backup singers' "ooh-la-las" because I was dreading and waiting for the chorus again. Like a roller coaster right before the big drop, everything slowed down except the pounding in my chest. Imran pointed to me on cue.

If this is what people feel like when I'm recording them, I don't recommend it. My palms are less sweaty on my side of the camera.

I started the chorus again and the band sang with me. Or I sang with them. And Umma and Mrs. Richardson echoed us. We got louder with every line until I couldn't feel the pounding of my heart even a little.

By the third chorus, the backups knew most of the words, joining in loud and off-key and perfect. And when they held the last note, all of us were laughing.

"You were wonderful, Sammy," Umma said.

Imran couldn't stop jumping in excitement, even after the song was over. Umma and Mrs. Richardson were already planning their moves for next time.

The drummer came over, her hair towering over me.

"You know, you are one cool little girl."

Me?

"You held your own out here. That's not easy to do."

"Umm, thanks," I said. "I really like your hair."

"Well, thank you right back," she said, patting her curls.

She held her knuckles for me to bump.

I did.

Another Non-invitation

My feet barely touched the ground on our way home, and my head buzzed.

"I was so good. We were so good," Imran said. "We should totally form our own band and we can charge for tickets and everything. Sammy could take pictures and make videos."

My phone vibrated with a text from Alice.

Everything okay?

My stomach squeezed like it had when Alice walked away with Kiera, but my mood was too high to let that image bring me down. I didn't reply.

"And Sammy," Imran said, "you were awesome!"

I was?

"Why does that surprise you, Imran?" Umma said. "Sammy's like Umma, and everyone knows Umma is sooo cool." She hugged herself and pretended to shiver, confusing *cool* with *cold* again.

I tried to pretend like I didn't care, but a smile forced its way across my face and lasted until I read the next text from Alice.

Do you want to partner up for Kiera's party tomorrow?

I didn't know about any party. My feet felt a little less light on the sidewalk, my head buzzed a tiny bit less.

Me: I don't think I'm invited

Alice: I'm sure she just forgot. It's a superhero pool party. I'll add you to the group text

She added me to a group with more than twenty other numbers. I had no idea who they belonged to or what they had said before I got there, like walking into a room where you were the only one who didn't know anyone. I didn't have to scroll through the unidentified numbers to know Alice already had more friends in my school than I did. The last time I tried to hang out with people when I didn't want to was at Hoop-Earring's house, and that had not ended well.

Alice: I added Sammy to the group

We might partner up for costumes

Like Batman and Robin

In the virtual world, at least no one could see how long I hesitated.

I typed,

erased,

typed again,

erased,

typed once more,

hit send.

Hi

Imran and Umma were already choosing the next song to perform, but I couldn't focus.

Kiera: Hey Sammy. Totally forgot to add you to the list but didn't think it was your kind of thing

Which was it? Did she forget to add me, or did she think it wasn't my kind of thing?

"Like they're even going to want us back for another song," I said to Imran, satisfied to see his smile get smaller like mine.

Alice didn't recognize Kiera's disses and cues: Or Gru and minions. Can we do bad guys too?

There was no way I was going to a pool party at Kiera's with a bunch of numbers I didn't recognize, with someone who didn't invite me or want me there.

Alice: Wait. We'll surprise you

The only surprise would be if I made it to the party.

Kiera: The biggest surprise would be if Sammy actually came to my party

I hated that Kiera knew me so well.

I would have to go now. Just to prove her wrong.

One Big Happy Incredibles Family

I love waking up in the middle of a good dream, feeling like everything is okay. Until you remember your family is halfway around the world, or realize you have a pool party at your toilet papering ex–best friend's house.

My dread was confirmed when I saw 123 new messages on my phone. Before nine a.m. On a scale of one to ten, my desire to go to this party hovered around a two. Better than getting my appendix out, but worse than making an announcement about yearbook in front of the whole school.

The last text had been sent seven hours ago. Didn't these people sleep? I skimmed most of them, but stopped to read the messages with Kiera's and Alice's names attached. Somewhere along the way, the two-person team of Alice and me had expanded to include Kiera.

The needle on my scale dropped from a two to a zero.

Based on the group chat, the three of us were going as the Incredibles. Kiera would be Violet, Alice would be Dash. Which left Jack-Jack for me. One big happy Incredibles family.

Me: Sounds good

I resisted the urge to send an emoji to let them know how I really felt. Rolling eye. Upside-down smile. Vomiting green face.

Alice: Want to work on our costumes together?

Did she mean all three of us? I most definitely did not.

Me: I'll figure something out. Meet you at Kiera's

I saw the three dots of Alice texting. They stopped. They started again. In the whole four days I had known Alice, I had not seen her second-guess anything.

Everything okay? Alice texted me separately.

What is the opposite of okay? Not okay? That didn't sound angry enough. I was beyond upset and firmly in angry territory. All I wanted was a quiet summer. Instead I was spending my day at a pool party I wasn't invited to, with seventh and eighth graders I didn't know. The hair-flipping, makeup-wearing strangers who liked to lengthen all their vowels, telling each other things like:

"Sooooooo, I looooove your hair."

"Waaaaaaiiiiiit, you'll never believe what I heard."

No one loved my hair or cared if I believed what they heard.

I googled costume ideas for Jack-Jack. Luckily no diaper, and I actually had a footie pajama in the right color. I just needed to print an *i* for the chest.

"No waaaaaaay. You still wear footie pajamas? That's sooooo cute."

I would have to say I bought one for the party. If they asked.

Me: Everything's fine. Just have some stuff to do

Alice: Excited to hang out together at the party

Me: Me too

My dream of the perfect two weeks of summer was dead. RIP, perfect summer. May we meet again.

32

Just Me and My Onesie

The party was at 4:00 p.m., and I was still hesitating by my front door at 4:05. I was guessing no one got to these things on time, and I didn't want to be stuck alone with Kiera, pretending we weren't best friends five minutes ago, waiting for the real guests to arrive. The invited guests. The hair-flip boys and the long-vowel girls.

4:15. I'd stay for ten minutes and come back home. To prove Kiera didn't have any power over me, even though we both knew she did. Besides, I had been working on the "My Community" video like Mrs. Markley suggested. I couldn't make a video about community unless I actually got out and participated in it. I would have to suffer for my art.

4:28. If I left now and took the short way, I'd be there at exactly 4:30, which was too round a number. I was so glad Umma was busy with Imran and didn't notice my very un-Umma-like indecisiveness.

4:36. A respectable time. I closed the door behind me, took a deep breath, and finally let go of the doorknob.

The squealing laughter and music got louder as I got closer to Kiera's house, and a sign on the front lawn had an arrow pointing to the side gate of the pool. "Fun," it said in big neon bubble letters.

Doubt it.

Five minutes. I'd stay for five minutes. The latch on the gate wouldn't catch, and I steadied my hand to make the door open. I was immediately hit with a water balloon, throwing me off-balance. The intended victim took a few steps back, and we both went down, her head hitting my nose.

"Oh man, I'm so sorry," she said, offering her hand and lifting me up. My superhero logo was soaked, the ink smudged.

"Your nose is tooooootally bleeding," the girl said. I touched the wetness under my nose and confirmed blood. "She's bleeeeding," she yelled again, in case there was one person on the far side of the pool who hadn't heard. Someone turned off the music.

"Hey! Are you okay?" Alice asked, running across the lawn. She was wearing a red swimsuit, with a little *i* for the Incredibles on the strap.

"Umm, you're wearing a swimsuit?" I said, looking at my own head-to-toe red onesie. A onesie I knew was too babyish for the privacy of my bedroom, but somehow expected to be a good idea for a party in the middle of the day.

I looked around, taking in the other costumes. There were Spiderman and Green Hornet eye masks; one girl wielded Thor's hammer while another cracked Wonder Woman's whip. But they all wore swimsuits.

I wiped my face, the blood turning the back of my hand red to match my onesie.

"Let me get some paper towels," Alice said, leaving me alone.

I had only been at the party for a minute before the laughter and music and fun totally stopped. That was a record even for me. I squeezed my nostrils together to stop the bleeding. This wasn't my first nosebleed. Not even my first one at a party.

I recognized some of the people from math and gym and improv club, but their faces didn't reveal if they recognized me. The girl from the yearbook signing, the one with the hoop earrings, wore a Wonder Woman headband. Leaving me stranded at the school wasn't superhero-like behavior.

"Sorry you missed hanging out with us the other day," Hoop-Earrings said, offering her plate of watermelon and cubed cheese to me and setting it down when I said no.

"I didn't know you were friends with Kiera," I said. Because I didn't. I would never have agreed to go over to her house that day if I had. Not that I had ever agreed. Not that I had ever gone.

"We weren't. That was the first time I had hung out with Kiera. She came over when you couldn't. Hope your diarrhea is better."

"Huh?" Articulate Woman. That should have been the superhero I came as.

"Kiera said you couldn't come over because you weren't feeling well. Because you get diarrhea all the time. My aunt has the same problem."

Kiera's high-pitched voice interrupted our conversation, and I missed my chance to correct the misunderstanding. "Weeeeeeeeeell, isn't this precious?" she asked.

"I didn't realize we were wearing swimsuits," I offered, feebly.

She was enjoying this a little too much. "What did you think people do at a pool party, Sammy?"

Alice cut through the crowds, paper towels in one hand, a bag of frozen peas in the other. I knew that half smile, that inability to look me straight in the eye. I hated that look. She felt sorry for me.

I wiped under my nose with the offered paper towel; some of the blood had already dried. I never knew how frozen vegetables played into a bloody nose, but someone always brought me some.

"Are you okay?" Alice asked again. "Has the bleeding stopped?"

I let go of my nose to check, and a small trickle tickled one nostril. I shook my head no.

"You probably want to go home, right?" Kiera asked.

I wanted to nod yes.

In a movie there would be one of two outcomes:

1. The girl would run out of the backyard, back to the safety of her room.
2. The girl would say something so witty and funny the whole party would see she was, in fact, cool like them.

I was definitely not the second one. I was trying not to be the first.

"Oh, I can't stay long anyway," I said. I held back the tears and the shaking in my voice.

"Want to sit down?" Alice asked, tilting her head to the folding chairs and table of food on the deck. The silence was overwhelming.

"I could eat," I said, like it was the most casual thing for me to be wearing a bright red onesie, face and hand covered in blood, downing Cheetos.

Whoever turned the music back on, I owed them big-time. Someone jumped into the pool with a whoop. A couple of people started talking again. Finally a few of my prayers were being answered.

Alice loaded chips and guac and cupcakes all together on a plate. She still hadn't made eye contact. I caught my reflection in the glass patio door and I could see why. Red onesie, logo smudged and crooked, bloodied hand clutching my nose. If I had seen this girl, I'd feel sorry for her too.

"Aaaalice," someone yelled, "we need you to finish the game."

I took the plate from her. "Actually, I think I'll take this to go," I said, walking back the way I had come, careful not to spill everything and attract everyone's attention. Again.

"I'm coming with you," Alice said. "I'm not going to have any fun without you anyway."

"Nah, you stay. Umma and I are going out soon anyway."

"Alice," someone yelled again. "Come on!"

She looked over her shoulder at them. "You're sure?"

"One hundred percent," I lied. "We'll catch up later."

I made it to the front of the house before the first big fat tear soaked my guacamole.

33

It's Trash

Umma and Imran fed mangos into the blender, and I was grateful their backs were turned to me.

The clock on the microwave read five fifteen. All that pain in thirty minutes.

"Billy is going to bring his son next time he comes to Mrs. Richardson's for band practice," Imran said, a couple mangos dropping on the counter before he rescued them into his mouth. "I hope he likes Legos. I think we're going to be best friends." He bounced on his toes with the anticipation. "I've never had a best friend before."

The sound of blender and crushing ice and laughter intensified my anger, and I stomped past them to my room, slamming the door shut.

I unclenched my fists once the pounding in my chest slowed down. The skin under my nose tightened with drying blood, and the onesie felt heavy. Every bit of energy was drained from my body, my neck couldn't hold up my head, and my eyes couldn't stay open. I lay down, already in pajamas. I think that is what they called a sick joke.

I woke up to a dark room and shadows I didn't recognize. I wiped the sweat behind my neck, and the room wobbled when I stood. Umma had left two thermoses and a note in front of my night-light. "I like cold drink in middle of nite. Like mango lassi. But maybe you want hot chocolate? I make that also."

Something about Umma's kindness made me cry all over again, and I crawled back into bed not drinking the lassi, or pouring a cup of hot chocolate.

The next time I woke up the sun was streaming through my window. I didn't want to look at my phone because I didn't know what I wanted to see—messages from Alice, or no messages from Alice. I tapped the screen awake, but it stayed black, not even a flicker of life.

I showered before going downstairs, trying to wash away the embarrassment and anger; I watched the water around the drain turn from pink to clear when I scrubbed my face. I stuffed and shoved until that onesie fit in the bathroom trash can along with the packets of contact lenses and tampon wrappers.

Conditions to the Condition

I carried both thermoses downstairs. "Thanks Umma, but I didn't get a chance to drink either last night."

Imran was at the kitchen table, writing a letter to Zaara. She would be back before the letter reached India, but there was no point trying to explain.

"I have a new best friend, Sammy. Did you hear?"

"Oh yeah?" I asked. "What's their name?"

"Well, I don't know that yet, but I'm meeting him today."

Imran was going to have his heart broken again. He thought Ethan was his best friend last year. Until he realized he was the only one not invited to Ethan's birthday party, to any of the birthday parties. I didn't have a best friend, but at least I knew.

"We can practice things to talk about, for when you're hanging out," I suggested. I could teach him how to make a friend even if I couldn't follow my own advice, like Mrs. Markley improving my pictures when she couldn't take a good photograph.

He looked up from his letter. "I know lots of things to talk about. I'm really good at talking to people, Sammy."

That was my fear.

His eyes flickered to Umma when her voice raised in excitement on the phone. I didn't understand many Malayalam words, but sometimes I could put a story together from the bits of English thrown in.

"Something-something-something, Sammy. Something-something friend." Had she heard already, through the Umma-network, that I had made a fool of myself at the pool party? But she wouldn't be laughing if she was talking about that.

"Can I use your phone to call Zaara?" I asked, shaking mine once more to see if it would come to life. Imran had a phone that could call five people and do nothing else.

"Yes." He smiled mischievously, putting down his pen. "But it will cost you."

My own words came back to haunt me. When I couldn't listen to another fact about beluga whales or another detailed description of weather patterns, I made him pay for my attention. He would clean my room or

144

fold my laundry in exchange for listening to his ramblings. I was teaching him life lessons, I told Dad when he said that's not how we treat family. But Imran had learned a little too well.

"Come on, Imran. I only need your phone for like fifteen minutes." I really wanted to talk to Zaara. I needed to.

"You can have it for fifty, but it's going to cost you."

Umma was deep in the middle of a story. She could go for hours, and Zaara could be asleep by then. "Okay, what's it going to cost me?"

"I need backup again for the new song I picked for Pete's band."

I remembered how good singing with them felt last time, but I sighed, pretending like I was doing him a huge favor. "Do I get to help pick out the song?" I asked, already knowing the answer.

He shook his head no.

"Do I have to wear a costume of any kind?" Last time I didn't ask the right questions and needed three showers to get green paint out of my hair.

He shook his head no again. "And no backing out if Zaara doesn't answer," he said. I had taught him the importance of an airtight contract.

"Fine." I dialed Zaara before he could add more

conditions to his condition. My own phone came back to life right as we sealed the deal. Logically I knew my phone was inanimate and wasn't out to get me, but sometimes I had to remind myself.

"By the way," he said, "Zaara's busy at dance practice, and can't answer your call right now." I almost threw his phone at his head.

35

Desi Omelet

U mma kept her phone tucked between her ear and shoulder while she cracked eggs into a bowl. Her hand was blurry with the speed of whisking. "Omelet," she mouthed, not asking what I wanted. An omelet was exactly what I wanted.

"Desi omelet?" I asked.

She covered the phone with her hand for a moment. "When Umma is cooking, all omelets are desi." She pointed to the green chili and onions on the counter. Umma never used a cutting board, chopping everything into her palm, directly over the pan. Having tried the method myself, I don't advise it. I had a visit to the emergency room, a lecture, and a scar down my palm as proof.

The first bite of omelet was the perfect blend of spicy

and warm. I had carried around a plate of tear- and blood-soaked guac and chips, but hadn't eaten anything since lunch the day before.

"I'll give phone to Sammy," Umma said, sliding her phone across the counter. "Your mom."

"Assalamu Alaikum, Mom," I said, my voice catching a little. Missing them, and the embarrassment of the pool party, twisted together.

"Walaikum Assalam, baby. We miss you so much."

"I miss you too," I said, wishing she were there. "How's all the wedding stuff?"

"Jam-packed." Which was not the kind of word she usually used. "You would have taken some great pictures. Yesterday at the flower market, today at the bangle store."

I thought about telling her about the video contest, about the clips I was putting together for "My Community," but I wasn't ready.

"You would have hated the rest of it, Sammy." She laughed. "All the parties and the dressing up." She wasn't wrong.

"What about Zaara? Is she having fun?" I knew for a fact that she wasn't.

She didn't pause before answering, like the question deserved no thought. "You know Zaara, she gets along with everyone and goes with the flow. She's having a great time." I knew Zaara, but I wasn't sure Mom always did.

Umma opened and closed drawers to find stamps for Imran's letters. The letters that weren't going to get there in time anyway.

"Did Zaara say that?" I asked. "That she's having fun?"

This time Mom paused for a tiny moment. Not long enough that anyone else would have noticed. "No, I guess Zaara never said that." Mom quickly changed the topic to me. "I hear you have a new friend in the neighborhood."

I wasn't sure I still did.

"Yeah, her name's Alice. She's pretty cool."

Probably too cool for me.

The doorbell rang three times on Mom's side of the phone, shrill and impatient. "Sorry, Sammy, but I have to get going. I'm so glad you're having a good summer."

She was wrong about both daughters. She just didn't know.

36

My Community

I looked over the notes Mrs. Markley texted after I sent her the second video, about "My Community." I didn't understand why the video didn't feel right when the clips were all taken in my neighborhood. That's literally my community.

Tell a story, Mrs. Markley texted.

Make it genuine, Mrs. Markley texted.

Focus on only one video at a time, so your stories don't get muddled, Mrs. Markley texted.

I arranged and rearranged the clips of Mrs. Richardson's toilet papering. I wish I had asked to film Pete's band. That would definitely count as part of "My Community."

Nothing felt right.

I put my toilet papering pictures back in. Maybe that's

what my video needed—some heart, some pain. Community wasn't always positive, after all. Ask the girl with the hoop earrings and dog poop on her front step. Or ask me at a pool party.

I took the toilet papered tree back out. What's done was done, but I got to decide what role it played in my videos, on me. I chose for it to have none.

That's My Name, Don't Wear It Out

"The sky here is so, so big," Umma said, widening her arms in front of her, as we walked to Mrs. Richardson's. She never asked me why Alice wasn't there or why I had gone to bed so early. There's a reason Umma is my favorite.

Imran rode ahead on his scooter, too excited at the idea of meeting his new best friend to walk at our snail's pace.

Umma's keys rattled as they fell on the ground, slipping off the knot at the end of her saree where she kept them tied. I had made that keychain for her in kindergarten using my first school photo. My toothless smile and curly mop of hair filled the first *a* of *Samira*. I looked so different.

"You were so cute," Umma said. She ran her finger over my name. "One day I called and you told me, 'Call me Sammy now. I'm not Samira anymore,' you told me with serious face." She stroked my braid. "You always knew what you wanted, and you always asked for it."

I never knew what I wanted.

I never knew how to ask for anything.

"Do you remember that day, Sammy?"

She tied my face back to the end of her saree.

Of course I remembered. Losing your name isn't an everyday occurrence. "Kiera thought I should."

"Kiera thought you should what?"

"Shorten my name. She thought it was confusing when people called us, because the end of our names sound alike." I remembered her saying that while we waited in line for the swings in kindergarten. *"Plus, your name is hard to pronounce, so I should keep mine."* The logic had seemed solid at the time.

I remembered being called Samira, but it had been a while. "Umma, I kind of miss my name."

She kissed me on my cheek. "Of course you do, Samira."

Imran circled back, waving a stick like a wand, pretending to cast some terrible spell on me. I didn't need his help.

"What song did you choose for today?" I asked, grabbing his wand-stick before he poked my eye, or his own.

"It's supposed to be a surprise," he answered.

Imran has never been able to keep a secret, not when he found out Mom and Dad were getting Zaara a car for her sixteenth birthday, or when he heard them planning a trip to Universal Studios for spring break. Accidentally letting us in on secrets is one of my favorite things about him.

"How about a hint?"

"A surprise is a surprise, Sammy. This one is for Umma."

"For me?" Umma asked, pointing to herself.

His face crumpled at having said too much. Umma is hard to catch off guard, and I couldn't think of a single song that could. If I asked once more, the truth would spill, like that glass of Flaming Moe he tipped over on that no-longer-a-surprise spring break.

"Fine." I allowed him to keep his secret.

Umma called out to Mrs. Richardson, making her presence known, before letting herself in, Imran close on her heels.

"I'll wait in the garage," I said, the only one of us three concerned by the lack of an invitation.

I should have gone inside.

38

The Reluctant Roadie

Pete's white van with the dented bumper and bullet hole–looking rust spots pulled up, and I immediately regretted my decision to wait in the garage. Being uninvited seemed better than being alone with the band. Clumsy conversation, or its evil cousin, clumsy silence.

I tried to go inside before they saw me, jiggling the doorknob that must have locked behind Umma and Imran.

"Sammy, right?" Pete asked, pulling his guitar out of the back of the van. "Ready to get to work as our honorary roadie?"

My hand was still on the doorknob, my attempted escape unmentioned.

"Umm, sure?"

I wasn't sure what a roadie did, but like taking pictures at school events, I knew having an assigned job meant fewer chances of not knowing how to act, fewer chances of attention being on me. Fewer was more.

"Roadies have to move faster," Pete said, and my feet responded.

Cool Drummer was crouched in the back of the van, searching through a box. Her hair was pressed against the roof, a tattooed unicorn peeked through the rips in her jeans, and her gray T-shirt was so faded the outline of Minnie Mouse was barely visible. She made unicorns, faded gray, and Minnie Mouse look cool.

I waited for Pete to hand me something or tell me what to do in roadie-approved speed.

"See those boxes with the wires?" he said, lifting a heavy speaker to the ground. "Leave them in the east corner of the garage. You look like a fast learner, so hopefully I won't have to explain again next time." He was gruff. Like I was the one asking him for a favor instead of the other way around.

Next time? I thought this was a one-time gig, already using the lingo.

"Yeesh, Pete," Cool Drummer said, "that's child labor."

Billy unfolded himself from the driver's seat. He hadn't shaved since the last practice and possibly hadn't showered. "Hiya," he said to me, before tilting his head to the sky and arching his back, stretching like the letter *C*. "Technically it's only labor if you pay them, maybe?"

He leaned back into the front seat. "Get off your phone, Leroy. You're going to be on your best behavior today." I was guessing Leroy was the reason for his dad's stubble and weary tone.

Leroy jumped out of the car, landing on Billy's foot, ignoring his dad's yelp as well as his instructions to get off the phone. This was the kid Imran was excited to see, the one he was already calling his best friend. A Leroy look-alike jumped out of the car behind him.

I sized them up since Imran wouldn't know how. Leroy was about the same height as Imran. His hair was buzzed short, his face was red and blotchy on his cheeks, and his nose turned up at the end so you could see up his nostrils. His shirt was too tight and too short, with his belly button smiling through. The fact that I knew he had an outie was more information than I was looking for in a first meeting.

"Off the phone, Leroy," his dad reminded him. "You, too, Dennis," he said to the clone behind.

Leroy didn't budge. Pretended like he didn't hear.

Dennis didn't look up.

Billy held both his hands out. "But Dad, I was watching the game," Leroy said, before slapping the phone into his dad's hand, with a sigh and a grunt of displeasure.

"Dude," Dennis said, turning in his phone, "you didn't tell me your dad wouldn't let us use our phones when you asked me to hang out today."

So they weren't twins, just weirdly looked like they were.

Oh, this would not do at all for Imran. Making a friend could be problematic, but when they came in pairs, the situation could be disastrous.

I was still holding the box of wires Pete had asked me to set down in the east corner. I had no idea which way was east, but made quick calculations based on the direction Umma laid her prayer mat. Leroy/Dennis kicked the walls, their shoes leaving footprints on Mrs. Richardson's otherwise pristine garage.

"This could be your summer internship," Pete said to me. I guess I had found the right east. "An unpaid summer internship."

I went back to the van for more boxes.

"Besides, I didn't come up with the terms. Your brother did."

The second box was heavier, and I set it down.

"Wait? What?" I asked.

Cool Drummer laughed. "Looks like she didn't know the terms. I've got a younger brother, too. They'll do that sort of thing to you, Sammy."

I didn't know if it was her low, rumbling voice, the Minnie Mouse shirt, or because I felt powerful holding the drumsticks she handed me that made me say it. "Actually, I prefer Samira."

Leroy burped. Dennis burped louder.

"I'm Noor." She stepped out of the van and shook her head, letting her flattened curls bounce free again.

"Well, Samira," Pete said, easily picking up my preferred name. "Your brother negotiated your muscle for his chance to sing a song with our band today." Which explained why he needed me to sing backup so badly. And also why he had locked the door behind him after he went inside. To keep me stuck in the garage with the band. Evil genius–level sneaky. I was impressed.

"Which song?" I asked. It had better be worth it.

Billy kneeled in front of Leroy to explain why you don't kick walls, his index finger jabbing the air in front of Leroy's nose. I was surprised his finger didn't get sucked into one of those nostrils.

Noor stacked her boxes. They were bright blue and metallic with big clasps. "'Never Gonna Give You Up,' by Rick Astley," she said. "Not our usual type of music. Hence the negotiation of his sister's brawn."

I laughed out loud. I'm not an LOL sort of person generally, but our family had a relationship with that song. A love-hate relationship. I understood why the surprise was meant for Umma.

"There's a story?" Noor asked.

I rolled a box into the garage. Noor's were the only

boxes with wheels. One more reason to like her.

"You've met my grandmother."

"Coolest grandma ever," Pete said.

Everyone stopped to listen. Even Leroy and Dennis stopped pushing each other to the ground for a moment. All the attention made me a little nervous. Just tell the story, I told myself.

"My grandfather passed away a few years ago. He was the opposite of Umma. He loved to sit inside, while Umma was outside. Loved to read while Umma liked to talk. Umma likes music with a beat, and my grandfather listened to Mohammed Rafi songs and ghazals." If they didn't know who or what that was, they didn't say. "Except when he heard Rick Astley. He listened to that song about a hundred times." All of them were smiling. Me too. "We love the song because it reminds us of Bappa, but hate the song because we heard it so much. Rick Astley and Gene Hackman movies were my grandfather's two unexpected loves."

"Booooorrring," Leroy said, covering his mouth in a fake yawn.

"Soooo boring," Dennis agreed.

At least I wouldn't have to find a creative way to get back at Imran for volunteering me. Hanging out with these two would be revenge enough.

39

Rickrolling

The back doors of the van closed with a final thud. "Twenty-two minutes," Pete said, checking his watch. "You only saved us two minutes. Do better next time, Roadie."

Twenty-two minutes was enough to make my muscles hurt, and I rubbed a sore spot on my shoulder. Being a roadie . . . for a band . . . that practiced in my neighbor's garage. That sounded like the most "My Community" thing ever.

Every summer we spent a weekend at a cabin on a lake, a lake with a rope swing. If I held the rope and stared down into the deep water, I spent the entire weekend nervous about jumping in. If I grabbed the rope and just went for it, I had the best time. "Do you guys mind if I record the practice?" I asked quickly, before I could chicken out, holding up my phone to show them how.

"Knock yourself out," Pete said, his voice annoyed and impatient.

Noor tucked her extra drumsticks in her hair. "Don't let him get to you. He's a total grump until he strums that first string. And then nothing but smiles."

The garage filled with a squeal. "Fix the damn amp, Billy," Pete growled. Obviously, he hadn't strummed that first note yet. Billy was busy taking the phone out of Leroy's hand for the tenth time. I knew what had come out of the box marked "Amp." I turned a knob, but the squeal turned to a screech. I immediately turned it the other way and the noise settled down. The garage echoed with the sounds of drums and guitar. Pete started to smile.

Mrs. Richardson and Umma opened the door into the garage, mid-conversation, mid-laugh. The cool air from inside dried some of the sweat on my forehead.

"Where's Imran?" I asked. I needed to yell at him before the song.

"He's coming. He said he needs a minute," Umma said. I bet.

"We know our positions, though," Mrs. Richardson said. "He wants you to stand between the two of us." So I couldn't punch him when he came out.

I propped my camera on a folding chair, checking the angles, the lighting, and the frame rate like I had been taught, making sure the band was in focus, making sure I was not.

When all of us were in position, Imran opened the door and walked to the microphone, like the main attraction. He saw Leroy and Dennis sitting on the box closest to the only plug point, their phones wired to the wall like leashes. Imran waved with both hands, huge smile on his face, but they stayed bent over their phones. "Hey!" Imran yelled, but there was too much noise in the garage.

He tapped Leroy on the shoulder. No one else was paying attention to their interaction, but I couldn't take my eyes off them. Leroy looked up, slack-jawed and drooling. I held my breath. *Please be nice to him, please be nice to him.* Leroy took in all that is Imran: the blue cape, the matching socks, the big grin, the double waving hands. I pressed my hands into my belly, waiting for what Leroy would have to say. *All you have to say is hi, Leroy. You don't have to be nice, but please don't be mean. Please don't be mean.*

Leroy laughed. "No way, buddy. No way. This is not happening." He pointed to Imran and then to himself.

"Not in one hundred years," Dennis added. Not that Dennis looked like he could count to one hundred.

I looked around to see if Umma had noticed, but Mrs. Richardson said she was inside, getting a glass of water.

My mouth had suddenly dried up too, and I struggled to swallow once, then twice, shoving the feelings down.

"Do you know yet what song he's singing?" I asked Umma when she returned. I wanted to tell her about Imran. I wished she had seen. She could have fixed things.

"No, he said it's big secret," Umma said, "but I'm excited."

I stood in the middle, tossed between the softness of Umma and the hardness of Mrs. Richardson as they practiced their moves. The garage had plenty of space. There was really no reason for us to be so close.

You can't mistake that drum intro for any other song. Umma knew immediately. She put her hand to her mouth, and her eyes filled with tears. It was hard to surprise Umma. She knew things about you before you knew them.

"We're no strangers to love," Imran sang, and I couldn't gauge his mood from his voice, but at least his shoulders were neutral.

Umma sang along under her breath. We had played this song a million times at her house. Bappa never sang along, but we'd see his foot tapping, and the corner of his lips turn up, and an occasional snap. Dad claims he saw him dancing once. None of us believe him.

When the time came for the chorus, Imran didn't

have to get us going. We belted it out. Even frowny Mrs. Richardson knew all the words.

"Never gonna let you down."

We pumped our arms like in the video. Umma and I turned at the right moment, and Mrs. Richardson caught on pretty quickly. For a band that thought they were too cool for the song, they seemed to be having a good time too.

"Never gonna run around and desert you."

Soon the three of us were doing our own thing, abandoning the synchronized moves, shuffling our feet any way we wanted, swinging our arms, accidentally hitting each other.

By the end of the song we were all laughing, and Umma was crying, but through her smile.

Leroy's back was turned to us, the charger still stretched taut to the wall. Dennis watched over his shoulder.

"Oh, Imran, your Bappa would have loved that so much. I'm too happy now."

She waved her hands like she was inviting everyone inside. "I want to make special meal for everyone." Making meals for people was Umma's favorite thing to do. Her way to celebrate everything. "Dinner at our house tomorrow!"

40

What Did I Say?

U mma was already planning the special dinner on our way home, all of us riding our high.

"It was worth it, right, Sammy?"

"Yes, Imran, it was totally worth it."

"I did good?"

"You did great, Imran." His smile was so wide I could count every tooth, even the ones in the back, covered in chocolate. I wanted to ask him about Leroy, but also didn't.

"And I have two new friends!" he said.

He brought it up, not me. Imran had spent a few minutes with Leroy after the song, long enough to learn his name but not much else. "Umm, did you like them?" I asked.

He was skipping around us in excitement. Seven

seemed too old to be skipping. I was glad Leroy couldn't see. "Too early to tell," he replied. I disagreed.

"Do you think they liked you?"

He stopped mid-skip to pick up a green button on the side of the road. "Why wouldn't they?" Imran asked. "I'm very likable."

I had seen Imran chase them around after we sang, trying to insert himself into their conversation. I saw them trying to ditch him. Imran never noticed.

Umma was listing all the dishes she was going to make, counting them out on her hand until she ran out of fingers. In India she had an army of people to help her.

"We can help, Umma," I said. Imran scrunched his face in irritation. Being on the receiving end of forced volunteering is never as much fun.

"Imran can drive me to the store and Samira, you can drive me back." She laughed at her own joke. Mom and Dad had arranged for groceries to be delivered every week for Umma. They hadn't factored in the feast Umma was planning. Knowing Umma, they should have. She had only invited four people, but there would be enough food for the entire neighborhood.

"Your mom wrote down names of people who could take me to store if I needed. I will call them when I get home. They can come for dinner too." I wouldn't have been surprised if the whole neighborhood did end up coming.

"So much to do," she said. "So much."

I knew Umma's feasts well. She always needed a second and sometimes a third table when there was no more room on the first. As soon as we got home, she turned the laminated pages on the color-coded, tabbed binder Mom had made for her. "Umma's Survival Binder" was written across the spine, but this was the first time she had needed it.

"Here it is," she said. The list was filed under "Umma's First Party." "Where to find extra tables and plates. Does my daughter know me or what?" She ripped the page out of the binder. Mom would not approve. "I can ask Henry Miller."

Kiera and I used to pull weeds for Mr. Miller. He always paid us extra and made us lemonade.

Umma called him, repeating her introductions and answers when he couldn't understand her accent or the jumble of words she used. Usually she could explain her way through things using gestures and facial expressions, but not over the phone.

"He's out of town for his daughter's wedding," Umma said. "Who else is on the list?"

"Mark Carter."

Kiera's grandfather. I don't think so. "Who else?"

Umma turned the page over. "That's it."

"I guess it will have to be Mr. Carter," I said, like we had a choice.

Umma had pick-ups and drop-offs arranged before I had a chance to think of another plan. Mr. Carter would take us to the store the next morning and, of course, he would also join us for dinner. If I started counting dinner guests on my hands, I'd run out of fingers soon too.

I accidentally dropped my phone when it rang, bouncing under the couch. I scrambled to answer the call, relieved there were no new cracks in the screen. The old cracks were familiar to me. Zaara's face was immediately comforting.

"Hey, Zaara, how's it going?

"Miss you guys," she said, not answering the question. She bit the inside of her cheek. "Umm, Sammy, did you tell Mom I didn't want to be in the dance?"

I thought back to my last conversation with Mom. "I don't think so." But I wasn't totally sure I hadn't said something. "Why?"

"She asked me like twenty times whether I wanted to be in the dance. Since you're the only person who knew, I thought maybe you had said something." She was fiddling with her earring again.

"I don't think I said anything." I didn't want Zaara to be upset. Didn't want her to be upset with me.

She laughed lightly, her fake laugh. "It's no big deal, I guess. I don't want to worry her."

"But you don't want to be in the dance, right?" I asked. "Why didn't you tell her when she asked?"

"It's just a dance, Sammy. It's not a big deal."

There was an uncomfortable pause. Zaara and I never had uncomfortable pauses.

"I can't remember if I said anything, Zaara, but I'm really sorry if I did."

"It's fine. No big deal." Zaara looked over her shoulder. "Listen, I'd better get going." She hung up, not waiting for me to say bye. I didn't get to tell her about the band, about my videos, about Leroy and Dennis. I didn't get to ask her how I could protect Imran's feelings.

It wouldn't have mattered, because it turned out the person he needed protection from, that person was me.

41

I Am the Worst

"Maybe Leroy and Dennis will be at Mrs. Richardson's tomorrow," Imran said. Grocery stores could sometimes be overwhelming for Imran, so he was going to stay with her when we went shopping the next morning.

I kept going back to my conversation with Zaara. I hoped she wasn't mad at me.

"I wonder which Legos we should start with," Imran said.

All I had done was ask Mom if she thought Zaara was having a good time in India. That wasn't like saying Zaara didn't want to be in the dance.

"One of these days Leroy and Dennis might even come over to play. You can meet them properly then."

I wished Imran would shut up. I couldn't hear myself

think. I sent Zaara a text explaining that I hadn't meant to tell Mom anything.

"When Zaara comes back, I'll ask her to make a cape for Leroy and Dennis as well. Then we can all have capes."

"Shut up, Imran."

I read the text I had just sent. The words didn't sound like I was really sorry. It was hard to concentrate when Imran wouldn't stop talking.

"Shut up, Imran!"

I tried to come up with better words for Zaara, tapping my apology/explanation into the phone.

Notifications streamed down my screen. Alice and Kiera, arms draped over each other's shoulders, tongues sticking out. Alice and Kiera spitting watermelon seeds into red Solo cups. Alice and Kiera pouting for the camera with wing tip eyeliner and bright red lips, cheeks sucked in.

"Hey, are you texting Zaara? Did you tell her about my friends?" Imran stood on the rungs of my chair to look over my shoulder.

"Shut up, Imran. Just shut up!" I stood up to get away from him, but his weight toppled the chair. He lay on the floor, tangled in the rungs. "JUST GIVE ME ONE SECOND." He was always under my feet, tripping me up.

"Geez, Sammy, why are you always mad?" he asked, rubbing the back of his head.

I wasn't always mad. Why was he always clueless? "Imran, they are not your best friends. Why don't you ever understand?"

He managed to unhook his legs and right himself and the chair, so I hadn't really hurt him. Yet.

"Dennis said we were friends. He wants to see my Legos." His confidence was irritating.

"News flash, Imran: he's not coming."

I probably would have been crying by then if I were him, but he stood there totally unbothered, his big eyes without a hint of tears.

"But he said he would."

Imran needed a dose of honesty and I was the only one brave enough to do the job. "He was lying. You don't have any friends, Imran, because you're annoying and you're weird. No one wants to see your Legos, no one wants to hear a million facts about Jupiter." My legs were planted wide and my body was tense.

"Zaara loves my Legos. She loves hearing about the solar system." We stood inches from each other, his stance reflecting mine.

"No, she doesn't, Imran. She's lying too. Everyone lies so they don't hurt your feelings, but here's the truth." I was going to set him straight. "You are never going to be invited to a single birthday party, never have a single playdate, never have a single friend," I said, my finger accentuating every word.

"You're the one without any friends, Sammy." The seven-year-old's comeback of "No, I'm not, you are" was true.

I poked him in the shoulder with each word. *"No. You."*

"Kids in school tell me I'm weird all the time, Sammy. I already know."

The anger from my still-pointing finger, from the balled-up fist, from the stiffness in my legs all melted, and there was nothing left to hold me up. Someone had already told him that? It was one thing for your sister to tell you the truth. It was a very different thing for kids at school to be saying the same thing. I took the deepest breath to expand my chest, so my heart would have space and wouldn't break into a million pieces.

"I don't know how to be any other way." He was still rubbing the back of his head. "But you, Sammy, you are the absolute worst."

I already knew that too.

42

An Apology

I wished Zaara and my parents were there, working on an annoying jigsaw puzzle around the table, pulling out a board game while I rolled my eyes. Making Imran feel better when his sister didn't know how.

Umma was on the deck reading her newspaper and Imran was tucked in next to her.

"I thought you'd already be busy in the kitchen," I said.

"Today I rest. Tomorrow all the fun starts." I had never heard Mom or Dad cook for a crowd and call it fun. Imran's head was on her lap, and she scratched his scalp in soothing circles.

I sat next to him. He ignored me. I deserved that.

I put my hand on his foot. He kicked it away. I deserved that too.

I sat still, waiting to figure out my next move. He

unburied his head from Umma to take a quick look to make sure I was still there, to see what I was going to do next. That was when I knew he was going to forgive me, even if I wasn't ready to forgive myself.

Imran was not the best at reading people's emotions. His school counselor helped make laminated square cutouts we hung on the fridge. Each one had a face with a different emotion. Mom and Dad would have to point to the angry one to teach Imran he had done something that made them mad. My face must have been cutout obvious in my guilt, in my sadness, because he stretched out his arm, palm up, and rested it on my leg. That had been his preferred method of soothing when he was younger.

He knew I was saying sorry.

I drew lines up and down his forearm with my fingertip the way he used to like. He hadn't let anyone do this in years. I started turning my lines into circles and squiggles when he didn't pull his arm away.

"I'm sorry, Imran," I whispered into his ear, embarrassed by my own behavior, that Umma would hear, that I had created the need to apologize to him.

"Okay," he answered. And we didn't have to talk about it again.

43

No Escape

Umma had been up for hours, having "fun" before our morning trip to the grocery store. Counters were covered with bowls of washed tomatoes, cut onions, peeled garlic, colanders of drying cilantro. The oven light was on for rising dough. Daal was soaking. Beans were sprouting. Science lab meets farmer's market.

"I can walk with you to Mrs. Richardson's house," I told Imran, still trying to make up for yesterday.

He was filling a tote with watercolors and brushes. "Sure, but if my friends are there I won't have time for you, Sammy." Imran wanted to learn how to paint, and Mrs. Richardson had agreed to teach him when I asked. Me from a week ago would never have imagined suggesting Imran spend one-on-one time with scowling Mrs. Richardson. Unless I was trying to get him back for something. But a lot had changed.

Alice was outside her house when Imran and I got to Mrs. Richardson's. She was wearing cut-off black shorts and a T-shirt with a band I had never heard of. Super tame for Alice. "Nice tote," she said. Zaara had made it for Imran to go with the cape. "Autism, that's my super-power" was written across it in big blue bubble letters.

"Thanks. Don't have time to talk. Got to go," Imran said, letting himself into Mrs. Richardson's house. Leaving Alice and me together. Alone. I hadn't seen her since the pool party.

"I'll walk with you, Sammy," Alice said.

"Thanks. By the way, I decided to use my real name again," I told her. "Samira."

"Samira," she said, practicing the sounds until we fell back to silence. We stayed along the edges of the lawns. The quiet felt heavy between us. I knew why. "Umm, so how was the rest of the party?"

Alice's phone buzzed in her pocket. "You didn't want to come to the party. I shouldn't have made you. I thought I learned that lesson already." Both of us were still avoiding eye contact. "I'm sorry I didn't. The whole thing was . . . awkward."

"Awkward?" I asked, trying to lighten the mood. "Awk-ward is spinach stuck between your teeth." She looked at me, and I didn't look away. "That party was death by onesie. I mean, what was I thinking?"

"Okay, it was kind of brutal," she said, through her giggles, " but I kind of liked the whole outfit!"

"Umm, of course *you* would," I said, referring to her usual over-the-top fashion choices.

And we laughed together, at each other and at ourselves.

"I'm going to the grocery store with Umma. But maybe I'll see you around later," I said, picking up my pace and waving goodbye.

She looked confused. "Umm, yeah. I know you're going to the grocery store. Kiera and I are coming as well."

Kiera was already at my front door. She was dressed the same-ish as Alice, in cut-off jean shorts, a concert T-shirt, and white tennis shoes. I guess dressing alike is fine if it's not a birthday shirt, in line at Build-A-Bear. Their faces had the same blue eyelids and black lipstick.

"We were working on a lipstick tutorial," Alice said. "What do you think?" She pouted for me.

"Nice and . . . black?" I offered.

I didn't understand why the two of them were coming, but I needed a plan to avoid what could only be a total nightmare.

Plan A: Pretend to be sick. Which would mean Umma wouldn't go to the store, and there would be no dinner party.

Plan B: Say I changed my mind about going. Which would mean Umma would have to navigate the grocery store without me.

Plan C: Go to the store, suffer through the assured nightmare, come back and crawl into bed.

"Ready to go, molay? I'm so excited to have a party. So many people in the house. I will feel like I'm back home."

Plan C it was.

"Yup, I'm ready." Not even close.

Mr. Carter pulled into the driveway, window down, white hair sticking out at all angles from under his green Packers hat. He had lines on his face so deep they could hold a penny. He had showed us once. He whistled along with the radio. Nondescript instrumental music. How fitting that my theme song was playing.

"Hello, girls!" Umma said, waiting for Alice and Kiera to separate so she could walk between. If she felt the tension I was oozing, she didn't let on. "So lucky I get so many young beautiful girls to take me shopping."

Kiera dusted off the back of her shorts. "We're thinking about having a sleepover tonight and wanted to get some snacks." Loaded nachos, triple fudge cake, snow cones, and cotton candy. I had been part of Kiera's sleepover snacks for years. I tried to not let my face give away how I felt.

"More people we have, the faster shopping will finish, and I can get back to my cooking," Umma said, going back to make sure the door was locked. "Thank you for coming."

Please don't invite them for dinner. Please don't invite them for dinner. Please don't invite them for dinner.

Alice slid across the back seat of the car while Kiera kept her hand on the door, waiting for me to take the middle.

"Did you watch the game yesterday?" Umma asked. How did she know that's how people started conversations in America? And what game was she talking about? Mr. Carter lowered the volume. "Let It Be"; I finally recognized the song. I wondered how Paul McCartney would feel about being my theme song.

"You watch soccer?" Mr. Carter asked, flicking the felt patch with the logo of a soccer team that hung from his rearview mirror.

Umma nodded. "I didn't know many people here liked to watch."

"I used to work in a stadium; that's how I got into it.

I'm glad the games are in South America this year so I won't have to wake up in the middle of the night to watch."

"And so lucky with the weather," Umma replied. "I went to Germany to watch the games when I was pregnant with Samira's mother. So, so rainy."

Mr. Carter turned the radio off. "Wow. Who did you watch?"

And just like that, they were friends.

Meanwhile, in the back seat, things were extremely different.

I shifted in my seat and held my muscles taut so my legs wouldn't touch Kiera's or Alice's, steadying them with every bump and turn while Kiera took selfies. Her pictures were never very good, making her look strange and strained. I was definitely not going to give her pointers.

"How's the toilet paper investigation going?" Kiera asked. "Alice told me all about it." I don't know if she was smirking or I imagined it.

"Nowhere," Alice answered over me.

It was true from her standpoint. We didn't have any momentum, didn't have any clues, didn't have any leads. From my standpoint, we had no desire.

"Big surprise," Kiera said.

I stacked my feet one on top of the other to take up less space. I fiddled with my phone, pretending to not listen to their conversation, the one literally happening over me, about me. A notification slid down my phone letting me know Kiera had posted a new photo of Alice and her in the car. She had managed to leave me out of the photo even though I was right there between them.

I swiped to delete the notification. I didn't need to see that sort of hell.

I was living it.

Lady's Fingers

The familiar drive to the grocery store had never required my attention before. Now I counted every mile, dreaded every turn that slid me into Kiera, prayed for every traffic light to turn green.

Umma and Mr. Carter had gone from World Cup to Germany to pound cake to gardening and landed back on World Cup by the time he reversed into the parking space.

Umma tore her list into two. "Kiera and Alice, since you two are so nice to help me shop, why don't you do this half of the list?" She folded the other half. "Hope you don't mind, Samira, but I need your help with the other half."

If I could have hugged Umma without looking like a baby, I would have.

"I'm going to get a haircut next door while you're in the store, if you don't mind," Mr. Carter said, walking in a different direction from the rest of us. Alice and Kiera slowed to read their list.

"So, Umma, what's on our end of the list?" I asked.

She unfolded the piece of paper and showed me a blank sheet.

"Umma never has list. It's all up here." She tapped her temple three times.

I smiled for the first time since getting into the car. "Then, what's on Kiera and Alice's list?" I asked, separating a grocery cart from the others and checking the wheels before offering it to Umma. She liked to push.

"I quickly scribbled list on the way here. How you call it? Wild geese chase?"

My smile turned to a laugh. "Wild goose chase."

She nodded.

I didn't want to ask why. Maybe she saw how uncomfortable I was in the back. Maybe Umma saw through Kiera's smiles and fake politeness.

"I'm selfish. I wanted only you and me today. I hope that's okay."

Okay? Safely out of sight from Kiera, I hugged her to let her know how much more than okay it was.

Umma picked through onions, smelled pineapples,

and squeezed tomatoes to her heart's content in the pro-duce section. "I need lady's fingers."

I had no idea what she was talking about. I wiggled my fingers at her. "Like these?" Umma pinched my cheek. Only Umma could pinch my cheek and not irritate me.

"No, silly. The vegetable."

"What vegetable, Umma?" I asked, reading names in the section that held fruits and vegetables I could never identify. Dragon fruit? Buddha's hand? Those are real things.

"I don't know other name," Umma said, "but it's this long, and this thick." She measured two of her fingers. "Can you ask someone to help?"

Some of my least favorite things in the entire world: telling a server they had gotten my order wrong, asking someone in the store for a different size shirt, and looking for someone to help at the grocery store. I have walked past people wearing the right-colored vests and name tags and lied to Mom that I couldn't find any-one. She would then monologue about how there were never people to help in stores anymore, and I'd be off the hook.

I was going to do the same thing. Lady's fingers sounded disgusting. I was doing all of us a favor.

Three grocery store employees were restocking the

freezer with Popsicles. You never saw them standing in groups. I was being mocked for trying to avoid them.

I heard that distinctive Kiera giggle. Alice playfully pushed her, which made them start laughing all over again. If they looked up right at that moment, and they were bound to, they would see me staring at them while they shared a joke. I looked pathetic. Not red-onesie, bloody-nose pathetic, but still.

"Excuse me," I said, but all three employees were too engrossed in their Popsicles. "Excuse me," I said a little louder.

The woman with hair a strange shade of red turned around, pursing her bright pink lips and touching her heart-shaped locket. She had dark spots along her cheeks. Not freckles, but rough, scaly spots. "Yes?" she asked, her tone clipped, her voice unfriendly.

"Umm. My grandmother needs help finding something in the vegetable section."

She put one hand on her hip.

"Now, please."

"And you couldn't find someone there to help you?"

I shook my head no and she sighed.

"Fine. What does she need?"

I looked over my shoulder quickly to see if Kiera and Alice were watching me. They were. I needed to create distance between us. "I'm not sure. My grandmother can tell you."

The woman kept her hand on her hip and made no attempt to follow me. "It's hard to help someone when I don't know what they want."

One of the other ladies stopped shelving to turn around. "Traci," she said, although redhead lady's name tag said "Mary." "Go help the kid out for god's sake."

"Fine," she said again. Not sounding fine at all.

45

Slimy and Offensive

Traci-Mary followed me to the vegetables, where Umma was still squeezing, sniffing, and sorting.

"WhaT can I helP you finD?" Traci-Mary asked, heavy on the last letter of her words in case the tapping foot and folded arms didn't make it obvious she didn't want to help. She had met her match in Umma.

"Oh, thank you so much," Umma said, returning her tone with kindness. "I'm looking for lady's fingers."

Traci-Mary uncrossed and crossed her arms, and leaned back a little. "I'm sorry. Can you repeat that? I can't understand your accent." She said it slow and loud like Umma was dumb.

Umma laughed. "I'm looking for lady's fingers. I don't know what you call it in this country."

Umma was doing fine without my help. At least that's what I told myself.

"Well, this is the only country I work in," Traci-Mary sneered, in that same loud, slow voice. A mom with a runny-nosed kid in her shopping cart stopped to see what the commotion was, both of their mouths slightly open.

Move it along, nothing to see here.

Umma kept going. "Lady's fingers are green, and thick here," she said, pointing to the base of her finger, "and thin here." She pointed to the tip.

Traci-Mary was practically yelling now, with a pause between each word. "I. DON'T. UNDERSTAND."

Umma ignored the attitude, the tone, and the volume. "When you cook, it takes long time because vegetable is—how you say it—vegetable is slimy."

A small group was forming around us now. Some had their phones recording, in case this turned into more. I hoped it wouldn't.

"Maybe she means those cookies you use for tiramisu," someone offered. "Those are called lady's fingers."

The woman with the baby in the shopping cart was still there. "She said it was a vegetable, not a cookie."

Traci-Mary took one step forward. "Maybe you need to try another store. We only know words we speak in *this* country." A few more people, with shopping baskets of Oreo cookies and carts with twelve-packs of Diet Coke, stopped to see what was going on. "There's a Mexican store a block down. *Try. There.*"

"You don't have to be rude about it," someone from the gathering crowd replied.

Umma didn't raise her voice. She didn't back down. There was no anger, but also no apology. Not even in her eyes. "My English not very good," she explained.

"No kidding," Traci-Mary replied. I saw Alice and Kiera join the crowd. Both their faces were confused at what was going on. Alice looked concerned.

I could have my tree toilet papered and not say anything. I could run away from the embarrassment of a pool party gone wrong. I chose silence when I didn't know how to keep the friends I wanted and get rid of the friends I didn't. I was used to being me, but I wasn't going to stand by while some woman with a bad dye job and wrong name tag treated Umma rudely. I wished I had googled what lady's fingers were instead of looking for Traci-Mary, really helping Umma instead of pretending to help. I had sabotaged myself yet again.

I crossed my arms like Traci-Mary, and spoke in the same slow, loud tone. "HER. ENGLISH. IS. FINE."

"Well, I can't understand anything you people say."

I moved to the gap between the two of them. I was eye to eye with ignorance.

"Well. Maybe. You. Should. Get. A. Better. Education." I couldn't quit talking that way, even though she had.

"If you decide to live in our country, learn our language."

Umma stepped forward to stand next to me, so I wasn't alone.

"Why? So she can sound as dumb as you?" I asked, forcing myself to stop the pauses, and lower my volume. "My grandmother speaks five languages. You barely speak one."

A big man stopped his shopping cart. I wasn't being rude, "a big man" is the best way to describe him. He towered over all of us, his chest like a barrel, his face thickened and discolored from the sun, his Harley-Davidson leather vest explaining why. "What's going on here?" his voice rumbled, deep and low.

Traci-Mary looked smug. "These people are looking for some sort of vegetable, and I'm trying to explain to them that we don't carry that sort of stuff."

His boots squeaked on the floor. I didn't uncross my arms, steeling myself against whatever was about to go down.

"Leave them alone," someone said, but no one stepped in, and they stayed behind their phones. For protection.

For avoidance. I had done the same many times.

"Are you Indian?" he asked, his voice rumbling.

I tried to nod but was unsure if my head moved.

"Any of you three speak Hindi?" he rumbled again.

"I do," Umma said. Like Traci-Mary, I was barely useful in one language.

He started speaking in what I could only assume was fluent and perfect Hindi. Umma replied. He said something back. Umma said something again. They laughed.

The gathered group looked at them back and forth like a tennis match. Traci-Mary had her mouth open. If only a bee would fly in.

"Okra," he said. "The vegetable she's looking for is okra."

Traci-Mary still hadn't closed her mouth.

"Get the nice lady some okra."

Traci-Mary had no choice but to go find the offending vegetable.

Umma and the man kept talking in Hindi, so the rest of us had no idea what they were saying. The crowd slowly dispersed. There was nothing left to see. Nothing left to live stream.

"We should go look for the things on our list," Kiera said.

"Are you okay?" Alice asked.

"Why wouldn't I be?" Kiera asked, opening the folded goose chase of a grocery list.

"I was talking to Samira," she said, tapping my shoulder.

I turned around on my heel, surprised to hear my name. "Yeah, I'm okay." I pulled my braid. "Thanks for checking."

"Umm," Alice said, stalling. "I'm sorry we couldn't find anything on your grandmother's list."

"Don't worry about it. Umma's spellings can make it tough to know what she means. One time—"

"Come on, Alice," Kiera interrupted, dragging her away.

"See you tonight," Umma said, finishing her conversaion with the man in the leather jacket. He waved back like a toddler, grabbing the air in front of him twice before his squeaky boots took him away.

"Samira, Samira, Samira," Umma said, bringing me into a tight hug, "Mashah Allah, you were so brave and strong."

I surprised myself by agreeing.

"Of course, I was not surprised," Umma said. "Not one bit."

Traci-Mary came back with a bag of okra. "Here," she said. Not politely. But not in that slow, loud voice.

"Thank you for the lady's fingers," Umma said, and we both cracked up laughing.

Umma and I waited in line to check out. "You invited him for dinner?"

"Of course." Like there was never a doubt or question.

"He's a stranger, Umma. He could come to our house and kill all of us." I had been warned about stranger danger since forever. We inched forward in line, okra triumphantly on the top of our cart.

Umma inspected the tomatoes she had chosen, smelling them. I didn't know tomatoes had a smell. "Fruit and vegetables look so perfect here. But I like the smell better in India." She put the tomato back in the bag, tying it with a knot. "He went to high school in Kodaikanal, Samira. That's neighboring state to Kerala." Like that explained why he couldn't possibly be a threat.

"But," she said, a moment's look of guilt on her face, "maybe we don't tell your mother how I meet him."

46

Take Up My Space

Alice and Kiera were already waiting by the car, and Mr. Carter turned the radio off when he saw us coming.

"Alice was telling me all about the grocery store excitement," Mr. Carter said, helping load groceries into the trunk. "You're quite the hero, young lady." *Hero* sounded like a bit too much, but I didn't stop him.

Kiera was quiet. No giggling. No sarcastic comments. She waited for me to get in the middle again.

"I'll take one of the window seats," I said, letting Kiera be the one with her knees pressed together and the middle bump digging into her back.

"Fine. Whatever."

"They did good job with your haircut," Umma said, and they picked up right where they had left off.

I let their voices fade into the background like a hum.

My leg fell to Kiera's side.

She shifted a little to give me room.

It felt good to take up some space.

Maybe I'd want to prove who toilet papered my house after all.

In Our Home?

"Don't unpack all the groceries, Samira, just bring inside," Umma said, leaving me with what seemed like a million bags in the garage. "Imran will be home soon. He can help."

By the time I dragged the last bag inside, pots were already on the stove, burners started.

"Also, Samira, I invited your teacher for dinner. Mrs. Markey."

"You mean Mrs. Markley?" An orange fell out of the bag I was carrying and rolled under a chair. I had never had a teacher in my house before. "How do you even know her?"

Umma double knotted her apron in front so I knew she meant business in the kitchen. "That day she dropped you after your yearbook. When you went to your room, she and I had nice chat. Very nice woman."

I didn't disagree, but I wasn't sure how I felt about her being in my house. Teachers belonged in schools. One summer I saw my science teacher at the swimming pool, and I got so confused I pretended like I didn't see him.

"Samira," Umma said with a wooden spoon in each hand. "Can you choose music for party? Make—how your mom call it—make a mixed tape of songs?"

"A playlist for the party?"

"Yes. Playlist. Also, you take photos of party, please." Umma knew which side of the camera I preferred. She had seen some of my videos. She loved hearing how I chose a shot, decided what parts of each video to cut, how I scrolled through all my different playlists until I found the perfect soundtrack. She dipped one spoon into a pot and brought it to her lips for a taste. "And Samira—"

I was already starting to move songs into a list I titled "Umma's Party Fever."

"Make sure you add the Hindi song with your name."

I was named after a Bollywood song. A song I had banned the day my name was changed to Sammy. Now I could play my name on repeat.

"How was the first painting class with Mrs. Richardson?" I asked Imran when he finally got there, conveniently after the last grocery bag was brought in.

His job for parties was always to make sure the good cutlery was clean, and he started laying out his supplies on the table. "Fun. After we painted, the band was practicing, so Leroy was there."

I wasn't sure I wanted to know the answer. "And you two had a good time?"

He looked at his reflection on the back of a serving spoon before sitting down to polish. "Definitely. He's going to come by to check out my Legos sometime."

"He said that?" Maybe I was wrong about Leroy. I picked up a polishing cloth and a silver fork.

"Yes, he said he couldn't wait to come play with me." Imran did a great job with the cleaning but took his own sweet time. He was still on his first spoon by the time I had cleaned three forks.

I stacked my forks on the cloth he had laid out. "What tone did he use?"

"Tone?" Imran asked. "What do you mean?"

That was part of the problem. Words could have so many different meanings depending on the tone. Leroy could have been sarcastic, threatening, or teasing, and Imran wouldn't know the difference.

"He said he wanted to come over and so he'll come over. The tone he used doesn't matter." Oh, it matters big-time. "He might even come over for dinner tonight with his dad."

Umma sang louder, the calm in the middle of her chaotic kitchen, leaving a plate of parotta and shrimp fry on the counter for us.

"You don't mind your first playdate being in front of a whole bunch of people?" I asked. Imran had never had a friend over. What if Leroy didn't like Imran's music, his capes, his million facts? What if he touched the wrong toys or broke his favorite one? Imran could lose his cool, have a meltdown, completely embarrass himself.

"Sammy, you're not cleaning them right at all." He took my pile of forks and moved them back to the first pile.

Leroy's dad didn't bring him to our house that night, but there was still a devastating embarrassment at the party.

Just not for Imran.

Arrivals

Everything was in place by the time the doorbell rang. The big table was extended like Thanksgiving dinner, plates set on banana leaves. Where had Umma found banana leaves? I'm sure Traci-Mary at the Highland grocery store would have no idea. The table was set for thirteen. If I were to invite everyone I knew for a party, five people might show up, three of them reluctantly.

Pete was there with Mrs. Richardson by his side. He was holding a small bunch of red and pink flowers that were already drooping. He wore a plaid shirt buttoned all the way up, and his bald head was shining.

"So beautiful," Umma said, handing them to me to put in a vase. "Thank you."

Mrs. Richardson held a tiny canvas, the size of a postcard, with fluorescent pink and neon green paint splatters and circles. "I haven't painted in years, but made this when I was teaching Imran."

"It's gorgeous, Dana. I know the perfect place in my house in India to hang this. Samira, can you take a photo?" I captured how proud Mrs. Richardson was by focusing on the crinkles around her eyes, and included the way she delicately held her end of the tiny canvas.

Imran dragged Pete to show him the Lego band scene he had put together. "This is you, Pete," he said, handing him the little yellow man holding a guitar.

Billy arrived next. Seeing him outside Mrs. Richardson's garage without his keyboard was strange. He had even shaved. "I come alone and I come empty-handed," he declared, arms wide open to show exactly what and who he did not bring. I was glad Leroy wasn't with him.

"You only have to bring yourself," Umma answered, ushering him inside.

"Leroy didn't come?" Imran asked. "I was going to show him all my stuff, the pictures I drew, my collection of dinosaurs."

"Sorry, Imran, but he's at his mom's house tonight. I'm sure he would have loved to come." Seemed unlikely, but I was glad for the lie.

The third doorbell was Harley-Davidson grocery guy. He brought a bouquet wrapped in purple, and Umma burst out laughing as she peeled back the tissue and saw okra, not flowers, tied together with red ribbon. He pulled one from the bunch and held it out for me. "And of course, for the star of the hour."

Me? The star?

"I'm Bodhi," he said to the others, who were already gathering around the trays of food on the kitchen counter. Umma's parties always revolved around the kitchen.

"Wow, you make Umma look even tinier," Imran said, with Bodhi towering over her.

He puffed himself up even bigger, Umma almost disappearing next to him. "'Umma' means 'mom,' not 'grandma,' right?" he asked. "How come you call her 'Mom'?"

"Zaara," Imran said, always explaining too much or too little.

"What he means," I said, "is Zaara heard Mom calling her 'Umma' and the name stuck." Umma pushed a plate loaded with pakodas and cutlets into his hands, and the room kept getting louder with conversations and clinking glasses.

When I opened the door next, Mrs. Markley was standing next to Cool Drummer. Two of my worlds were colliding, but there was no explosion, just small talk and introductions.

"Sammy," Mrs. Markley said, "so great to see you. So nice of your grandmother to invite me." She handed me the white box she was holding. "I brought a cake." I hoped it wasn't black forest. "Looks like a great opportunity to add things to your second video," she said, looking around at the guests who had already arrived, taking it all in.

"Way ahead of you, Mrs. Markley," I said, holding up my phone.

I knew my nickname for Cool Drummer was perfect, even if I only called her that in my head. Noor wore a long dress of pink sequins with jeans underneath and her head was wrapped in a big blue turban. "We got you a gift, Samira," she said, unzipping her knee-high boots at the front door.

"We?" I asked.

"The band." She unrolled the plain black T-shirt tucked under her arm.

"Nice?" I said, because being rude to guests is one of the only unforgivable sins, according to Umma.

She flipped the shirt over, revealing the word "Roadie" in big white letters on the back.

"Nice!"

"It's official now," she said.

Mrs. Markley's sandals had straps that wrapped up her legs like a Roman god's, and she finally managed to undo them. We should have considered adding a warning about shoe removal to the invitation. "Sammy . . ."— and she stopped herself when she heard the others calling my name—"or do you prefer Samira? You're part of a band! I can't wait to hear all about it."

The doorbell rang again and Noor and Mrs. Markley followed the smell of kheema puffs to the kitchen. "I'm so lucky your grandmother asked me to take her to the grocery store," Mr. Carter said. "Happy to be invited!"

Umma cleared shoes away from the front entrance with her feet.

"This is my wife, Sarah." Mr. Carter introduced Kiera's grandmother as she held out a bottle of wine with a red bow tied around the neck.

Umma accepted the bottle from her. "Thank you so much for bringing gift, but we don't drink alcohol."

Mrs. Carter smacked her forehead with her palm. "I'm so sorry. We should have known."

"No problem at all," Umma said, leaving the bottle on the entry table. "You take it when you leave, enjoy with your family. Think as gift from me." And she winked at Mrs. Carter, which put her at ease right away.

I counted eight guests, and three of us, which was the crowd I expected. I didn't get a chance to ask Umma who the others would be. I wouldn't have been surprised if she invited Traci-Mary from the grocery store. It's the kind of thing she would do.

When I opened the door next, there was a face I

couldn't quite place. "Package for Sammy?" he said.

Of course. Our mailman. But with a package for me? At night? And he wasn't even in uniform.

"Ummm . . ." I said, all those thoughts running through my head.

"I'm kidding," he said. "Your grandmother invited me for dinner."

Of course she did.

The house was warmer and even louder now. Cutlery fell on the floor; laughter filled the kitchen, Umma's loudest among them; and Imran competed to be heard, thrilled to have new victims for his endless trivia.

"Samira," Umma said, refilling plates before they were close to empty. "That's all the guests I've invited, but I leave Imran's friend's place there. In case."

"In case what?" I asked.

"In case you wanted to invite someone."

"You mean Alice?" I asked. "She's supposed to be having a sleepover with Kiera tonight."

She tucked a few stray hairs back into my braid and kissed my cheek. "Up to you if you want to invite. Up to her if she wants to come." She was already moving on. "Your glass is empty, Pete. You have to try another glass of my punch. It's world-famous, you know."

49

An Invitation from Me

My grandmother's throwing a dinner party, I texted, *if you want to come.*

Alice already knew about the party, of course, and knew we would be serving okra. This party would be nothing like one of Kiera's. The two of them were probably in the kitchen making inside jokes and pasta. I immediately regretted asking.

I saw the three dots of reply. Would she say yes?

The three dots disappeared. If she was going to reply.

The three dots appeared again. A polite no?

The three dots stayed. An impolite no?

I willed the dots to turn to words, feeling silly for inviting her when she probably had better things to do.

The doorbell rang and Alice stood at the doorstep red-faced and breathless.

"Hey," I said, as casually as I could. Like I hadn't gone through multiple stages of self-doubt a few moments ago.

"Hey." She was bent over with hands on her knees, her breath choppy. "I saw your text and started to answer, but decided to come over. Hope that's okay."

"Thanks for coming." I flicked an invisible particle off my leg, because that's what people do when they're trying to act casual.

"Umm. That grocery store thing today was kind of cool, right?" She shifted her weight to the other foot. I hadn't invited her inside, and she didn't invite herself in for a change. "I'm sorry I didn't stand up for you more." Alice had self-doubts too. She faked a laugh. "I didn't want to go overboard." That's never been my problem. "But you were awesome today."

I opened the door wider for her to come inside. "Thanks," I replied, happy I had asked her. "I'm glad you came."

She kicked off her shoes next to the others, her socks without holes. "Seriously? I was so excited to see your text, I ran right over, before you changed your mind."

"Before I changed my mind?"

Alice's wild lipsticks and green eyelids were no longer surprising to me. "Honestly, Samira, I wasn't sure if you wanted to be friends." If I thought someone didn't want to be my friend, I would be too embarrassed to say it out loud. "You know, this is the first time I haven't had to invite myself over." She realized she did that. "You've never invited me to hang out before."

I'd never realized I hadn't done that.

She hugged me tight. "I'm so glad you did."

50

Mistake Number One

The conversation moved from kitchen to dining table, and having Alice by my side made me less uncomfortable in my own home.

"Okay, Bodhi," Umma said, bouncing around the kitchen, happy to have the house full. "Use your muscles for something good. You can carry the biryani to the table."

He blushed and smiled, using the potholders with bunnies on them to carry the big red pot to the table. No one in our family had a particular attachment to little forest animals, but you wouldn't know that from the amount of bunny-themed stuff we owned.

"Find a seat, get comfortable," Umma said when everyone was milling around, commenting on the number of dishes squeezed onto the table, fanning the smells to their noses, "and most important—start eating.

"Eat," she ordered again, mobilizing everyone to reach for the dish in front of them, steam lifting from serving platters as they were uncovered.

"Why do you have a basket on your truck?" Imran asked, scooping raita by the spoonful. He liked a little biryani with his plate of raita instead of the other way around.

"So we can reach the electricity lines way up high when they need to be fixed," Pete replied. "I love it up there when there's good weather." He took a naan from the basket passing in front of him. "I'll sometimes sit up high and write songs once the work is done." I had never heard Pete string so many words together. Grunts threaded together, sure.

"And you used the basket to clean the toilet paper from the very top of our tree," Imran said.

"Your house was toilet papered?" Bodhi asked. "Kids are still doing that sort of thing?"

"Yeah." I nodded. For the first time, I didn't feel a sense of dread and didn't feel like I wanted to dig a hole and fall into it at the mention of the toilet papering. "I have pictures."

"Samira takes beautiful pictures." Mrs. Markley poked her cheek with a kebab when she took a sip of water.

"She's the photographer for the school yearbook."

Umma returned from the kitchen with a platter of eggplant she had forgotten. It wasn't unusual at one of Umma's parties to find an untouched dish on the counter after all the guests had left. "She's been taking beautiful pictures and videos all over neighborhood too."

The whole table responded at once, wanting to see "my work," as they called it. Like I was a real artist.

I shifted in my seat. "It's not good enough to show everyone."

"I disagree completely with that statement," Mrs. Markley said, kebab safely on her plate. "I've said it before. You're a natural. You should share your photos with the group." She fell back into teacher mode.

Mrs. Markley's comments, Alice by my side, Bodhi calling me a star, and a belly full of my favorite foods gave me the confidence I wouldn't have felt otherwise. "Okay, maybe I can share a few."

"You should hook up photos to TV so we can all see on big screen," Umma suggested.

Mistake number one.

51

Mistakes Number Two . . . and Three

"This is so lovely," Mrs. Carter said as we cleared the table. "We don't get to see our neighbors this much anymore." Everyone mumbled in agreement. "Remember when the kids were younger and we would have those block parties? With food and games and bubble machines and a fire truck?" She rested her stack of plates on the table. "I miss those days."

Parents loved talking about the good old days. Grandparents were even worse.

"We would use a big sheet for a screen and play a movie," Mrs. Richardson said. "All the kids would fall asleep outside. I think they watched *Home Alone*."

"I've heard my grandmother talk about those block parties," Alice said. "They were her favorite thing about the neighborhood."

"Those parties were wonderful." Mr. Carter collected wadded-up napkins, leaning against the table as he stopped to remember.

"All of you are stuck there like flies, and table is honey," Umma said. "You still have to eat dessert. Samira, set up photos for everyone to see."

Alice and I shifted furniture to face the TV. The room was small and all the chairs and floor cushions created a tight web, hard to get into, hard to get out of.

Mistake number two.

I selected photos from the ones I had taken around the neighborhood, no longer able to tell which ones were good or bad. Umma was ignoring everyone's pleas about being too full, filling bowls with payasam, serving pieces of Mrs. Markley's triple-layered chocolate cake, shooing everyone out of the kitchen when they tried to help load the dishwasher.

I started a slideshow of my photos. There was Pete curled over his guitar, eyes closed, Noor with her arms in the air right before she hit the cymbal, and Billy with hands blurred with movement over his keyboard.

"Wow," Noor said. "We look good!"

"She has some great videos she's been working on too," Mrs. Markley said with a sparkle in her eye. "Maybe we can convince her to show us."

Heat prickled at the base of my neck. "No, they're not good at all," I answered, bending my head over the phone and swiping through the photos, hoping she'd let it go.

"There's something about the videos that you didn't like, Samira. Maybe this very supportive group can give you some helpful feedback," Mrs. Markley suggested. The crowd whooped.

I guessed that made some sort of sense. "I have two videos I could share . . ." The guests whooped again. "One is supposed to represent my idea of 'home' and the second one is all about 'community.'" I tried to sound more confident than I felt.

Two-minute videos felt like twenty, and when they were over, everyone clapped more enthusiastically than I deserved. If there had been enough space to stand, I would have gotten my first standing ovation. I understood the cheering was more for me than my videos, but it still felt good.

"That's amazing."

"I love all the details in the first one."

"Hey, we were in the second video."

"How did you get that shot from the roof?"

"But why aren't you happy with the videos, Samira?

What do you think is missing?" The last question was, of course, from Mrs. Markley.

I twisted the charging cord around my finger. "I don't know. I guess it all looks too perfect, like everyone is happy all the time. And that's not the truth," I said.

"I get what you mean," Pete said, scraping the last bits of payasam from the bottom of his bowl. "You feel uncomfortable when you're not being honest. I feel the same about music."

The tip of my finger turned red as I twisted the cord tighter. "I added pictures of the toilet papering but then took them out. I can't decide if that helped balance the video or made it worse."

"Why don't you show us the pictures? I come here almost every day, and I didn't get to see the famous toilet paper–covered tree." The mailman leaned forward, elbows on his knees.

"They're on my computer, but I could get them," I offered, giving Imran my phone so they could continue looking at pictures until I returned. The mailman had to get up, and Noor tilted her chair on two legs, and I had to crawl between Mr. and Mrs. Carter to get out of the tight rings we had created.

Leaving the room—mistake number three.

I tripped over a pile of books in my room, falling on

my knees, almost crushing the laptop. The room was quieter when I came back.

Uncomfortable.

Twitchy.

"Swipe the other way, Imran," Noor said.

Imran held my phone with both hands, tapping too quickly with his thumbs. "I'm trying. The phone's stuck."

I heard Kiera's voice, but she wasn't in my living room, she was on the TV.

There were a lot of videos of Kiera on my phone; only a few were from this year. She had wanted to record her moves during our first dance practice, to see how she looked. That would have been fine. That wouldn't have made me want to claw my eyes out. The conversation I had with her after, the conversation playing on the screen for everyone to hear. That did.

"Are your parents coming to the talent show?" Kiera asked, repeating the move she was working on, swiveling her arms as she looked at herself in the mirror.

"No," I answered, "they couldn't change their flights. They're leaving for India that day." I could see bits of me in the mirror reflection. There's a reason I never liked to be on that side of the camera. I looked eager, like a puppy dog, less cute, more pitiful.

Kiera wasn't paying attention to me, but I hovered, hoping she would. "I bet you're relieved," she said. "My mom is pushy, but your parents are so . . ." She paused here, and I couldn't remember what she'd said until I heard the words. "So different."

I didn't remember this video, this conversation, but there was undeniable proof playing for all of us. "Imran, turn that off!" real me yelled at TV me, as I tried to get to him, to the TV.

"I'm trying," Imran yelled back, tapping and swiping with no result.

"And my grandmother will probably want to come," TV me said, annoyance in my voice.

Kiera turned around so the camera showed her face directly, instead of the mirror reflection. She put her hands in front of her like namaste, nodded her head side to side and used the worst possible imitation of an Indian accent. "Are you embarrassed of her also? Does she also smell like curry and wear funny clothes?"

"Hey!" TV me said, a moment of defense in my voice. The only moment.

"What?" Kiera said, dropping her hands and the smile on her face. "You're so sensitive. I'm just teasing."

The rest of this conversation I did remember. "Turn it off, Imran." Everyone was quiet and I felt like I was trying to get through maple syrup as I pushed my way to him.

"Where's the remote?" Alice looked behind her. Bodhi looked under the cushion he was leaning on.

"You think my parents are bad, wait until you meet my grandmother." TV me namaste'd my hands and bobbed my head like Kiera had, showing her how relaxed I was about the whole thing. Wanting her to like me so badly. "She is so embarrassing. She can barely speak English but tries to be friends with everyone." I grabbed the phone from Imran, my shaky hands punching in the wrong passcode to open the phone and disconnect the stream of embarrassment. "Everyone eat," I said in my Umma imitation, head still bobbing, accent thickened. "Whole world love smelly gross Indian food." My phone finally unlocked and I turned the video off.

It was pin-drop silent in the room. No eating, no movement, no breathing. The silence was too thick, the weight on my chest not letting me turn around.

"Samira," Umma said, her voice heavy with disappointment. The room behind me felt far away. "You're so funny. Your Umma imitation is my favorite." She fake-laughed.

I couldn't get myself to do the same.

Cereal for Breakfast

I tossed and turned all night, tiptoeing into the hallway when I heard the kettle and the familiar noises of Umma's morning routine. I stood in the dark of the stairway, watching her wipe away water drops from plates before stacking them in cupboards. There was no sway in her hips, no hum under her breath. The stair creaked when I shifted my weight, and Umma looked up. "Samira?" she asked.

"Yes, Umma," I replied, quietly.

"Why you creeping on the stairs?" She smiled. "Come have some breakfast."

I wanted to apologize. I needed to apologize.

"I'll get myself a bowl of cereal," I said.

"Okay, molay, if that's what you want."

Never, in all my life, had Umma let me have cereal for

breakfast, not without a fight.

Imran came down yawning, scratching his belly, heading straight to his Lego table. "Umma, you throw the best parties. I stayed up so late!" Satisfied no one had disturbed any of his structures, he returned to hug her. I wanted to hug her too. "Wasn't it awesome, Sammy?"

For once I was grateful Imran was oblivious about awkward situations, whether created by him or not.

I shuffled quietly around Umma, reaching for my cereal bowl, grabbing a spoon, doing a quiet little dance trying to avoid bumping into her, avoid looking at her.

My phone buzzed with a text from a number I didn't recognize.

Hope the new T-shirt fits. We need our roadie in a couple hours. You free?

It must have been Noor.

Me: Noor?

Noor: Umm. Who else?

I wanted to stay in the house and mope all day, replaying the worst part of the evening, but I also couldn't stand this strange distance I had created between Umma and me.

Me: Can I bring my friend from last night?

Noor: Sure. As long as she can lift things.

"Pete's band is going to play. You want to come,

Imran?" I asked, really directing the question to Umma.

Imran yawned again. "Nah. I have too many leftovers to get through. Let me know if Leroy is there and I'll come over."

I swirled the cereal with my spoon, watching the milk turn chocolate brown. "Umm, what about you, Umma? You want to come?" Did this count as an apology?

Her voice was gentle, and somehow that hurt more. "Thank you, Samira, but I have so much to clean up still. You go have fun."

The stone in the pit of my stomach felt like I would never have fun again.

53

Finally, The Halloween Incident

"Hey!" Alice was already waiting for me and the band on Mrs. Richardson's steps, where we had first met. "That was so much fun last night." She wore a puffy dress, in stripes of every color of the rainbow, ballooning out from the waist and cinching together at her knees, one pink high-top Converse, one green, like a box of crayons had exploded.

"Yeah," I said, still aching from Umma's hurt, "except for that video."

"Yeah, that was brutal." I wasn't sure I was ready for that sort of honesty. "What's the deal with you and Kiera, anyway?" she asked, measuring her words.

I measured my words back. "We used to be best friends." I shifted my feet uncomfortably before sitting next to her. "Even before preschool. All the way until this year."

"Whoa," Alice said.

Yup. Whoa.

I had known she was going to ask. I mean, who wouldn't? The Halloween Incident was almost eight months ago and I still didn't know if I was ready to tell anyone.

"So, what happened?"

October 31 was the worst day of my life. Worse than red onesie day. Worse than being abandoned in a Build-A-Bear line. I'm not sure if it was worse than the day I broke my grandmother's heart. The jury was still out.

"Because it was Halloween?" Alice asked.

"Yes, it was Halloween. But not because of that."

Every year Kiera and I had a Halloween party at my house. I loved Halloween because anyone could celebrate. Costumes and mini Reese's didn't care about religion or culture or skin color. I was thrilled Kiera still wanted to throw a party with me. Seventh graders didn't have parties with games, she reminded me for the hundredth time, in case I embarrassed her. No toilet-paper mummies, no marshmallow tosses, no pumpkin carvings.

"This year I want to invite a different type of people than we usually do," Kiera said. In fifth grade we invited all the kids in our class. In sixth grade we invited all the kids in our homeroom. I remember her saying *type* because the word made me wonder what *type* of person I was.

"Like who?" I asked.

We were sitting at my kitchen table, putting together trick-or-treat bags for Mom. She had tried to use the leftover Valentine's bags, but that's where I drew the line.

"There are a couple boys in math that are kind of fun." Kiera put two M&M's packets in a bag and I took one out when she looked the other way.

"Boys my parents don't know at our party? You know my mom will never, not in a million years, agree to that." Kiera was smart enough to be in math class with eighth graders. "Eighth grade boys? Never."

She bit her lower lip. "Umm, I thought this year, just this once, we could have the party at my house?"

She passed me a full bag and I twist tied it closed. "But we always have it at my house."

"I know," she said, forgetting to add a Twix. "But seventh grade parties are different, Sammy." She said my name like I was a child and she was not.

"Umm. I guess."

"Did your parents say okay to the party being at Kiera's house, with boys?" Alice asked.

"Not really."

I would have to lie to them. Sure, I had lied to them

before. About not brushing my teeth when I was too lazy. About saying I had prayed when I hadn't. About stuffing things into my closet when they asked if I had cleaned my room. I had never lied ahead of time, though. Never planned a lie.

The day before the party, I went to help decorate. Halloween night was going to be perfect. There would be a full moon. The thirty-first fell on a Saturday. Most importantly, there was no snow. Even with the lies and the change in venue and no fun games, it could be a good party.

Kiera had a few events planned ("We don't call them 'games,' Sammy"). We were going to throw ping-pong balls into cups on a table, tell scary stories around the fire pit in the backyard, and finish with Truth or Dare. I had terrible aim, I scared easily, and I didn't like the pressure of a truth or a dare.

I tried to sneak down the basement stairs, hoping Kiera's mom wouldn't see me.

"Hello, Sammy," she said, as I was about to close the door. "It's polite for a guest to greet people in a home they enter." Her words pulled me back up the stairs. Mrs. Carter always wore high heels, even inside the house, and her smiles were tight, never reaching her eyes, her forehead frozen.

"Hello, Mrs. Carter." My spine straightened and I pulled my shoulders back before she had a chance to tell me to do so.

Everything is always in perfect order at Kiera's house. "A place for everything and everything in its place," Mrs. Carter would say if I left a plate on the counter for even a second. I think that's why Kiera liked to hang out at my house. Or used to.

"She sounds like a nightmare," Alice said.

"Worse," I answered.

"What are your plans for Christmas this year?"

Mrs. Carter knew we didn't celebrate Christmas. We did the same thing every year. We had Indonesian food, Imran knocked down about ten chicken satays, and we watched a movie.

"The same as always, Mrs. Carter." She preferred I finished every sentence with her name. I wasn't sure why.

"Maybe your family should try some of the local traditions this year. Bake cookies, put up a tree, hang lights to brighten your house."

I didn't know how to answer, so I nodded.

"Yes, Mrs. Carter?" she suggested.

"Yes, Mrs. Carter," I replied.

"You may be excused, Sammy."

I escaped down the stairs before she had a chance to change her mind.

Downstairs, Kiera had been hard at work. The basement looked beautiful. There were twinkle lights in orange and black and cobwebs in the corner with spiders hanging from them. The beanbags were decorated to look like jack-o'-lanterns.

"Oh wow, Kiera." I turned back for a second look when I passed a skeleton. "Did that skeleton actually blink?"

Kiera waved me back up the stairs behind her. "Oh yes it did, and wait until you see the fire pit."

We ran past Mrs. Carter. "Slow down, girls. We walk in the house. We run outside." We both did a quick-walk to the backyard. The fire pit was full of little skulls, their eyes glowing. "I mean, how cool is that?"

I had to admit it was pretty cool.

"And I've got another secret," Kiera said when we were back in the basement. She lifted the bottom of the curtain to show me. Three bottles of root beer were hidden underneath, the necks dripping with condensation.

"Root beer?" Mom had finally broken down and let me have soda instead of juice boxes at last year's party, so I wasn't impressed.

She rolled her eyes at me. "No, Sammy, that's real beer. I took a few from the fridge."

"NO!" Alice said.

"It gets worse," I answered.

I counted the many lies I had told my parents, trying to convince myself that leaving out the truth wasn't the same as telling a lie. As long as I didn't do anything wrong, I shouldn't have to worry about who was coming to the party, or what was hidden under that curtain.

I checked and rechecked my costume a few hours before the party. I had a hooded robe, and a mask that turned my whole face into a single eyeball. Comfy and scary, my favorite combination.

Mrs. Carter opened the door in head-to-toe emerald green; monstrous red eyes on coils bounced around above her head.

"It's not polite to stare, darling." Her voice had no ups, no downs. It never did. "I'm a snake," she said, but didn't open the door wider to let me in. "I'm sorry," she said, even though her tone held no apology at all. "Kiera was supposed to let you know."

She could have kept explaining, but instead waited until I asked. "Let me know what, Mrs. Carter?"

"We're not comfortable having you at the party tonight." She exaggerated a pout, like the reason for the sadness had nothing to do with her. "I'm sorry," she said again, when it was so obvious she was not.

"Noooo," Alice said. *"Why?"*

"I'm getting to that."

"I don't understand," I said, forgetting to add her name to the end of my sentence.

"I meant to call your parents this morning, but I've been so busy, you know?" The bouncy eyes above her head jiggled and shook even though her own eyes were still.

I had no idea what she was talking about. Like none. "Is Kiera not home?"

"She is," Mrs. Carter said. "But she's busy setting up downstairs for her friends. Maybe she can explain once the party is over?"

I cursed myself for holding my mask instead of wearing it. How many times had I wished for a paper bag over my head when speaking to Kiera's mom?

"Do you need a ride home, dear?" she asked when I stayed frozen at her front door, rubbing the edges of the rubber mask like a genie's lamp. "Before Kiera's friends get here?"

That's when I finally understood I wasn't invited, that I was being asked to leave.

"From your own party?" Alice asked. *"I can't believe it!"*

"I couldn't either."

I kept standing there in my robe, focusing on her bouncy eyes so I wouldn't have to look at her real ones, waiting for things to make sense.

"You can wait inside if you'd like."

I shook my head no.

"You didn't ask her why?"

"I've never had a grown-up tell me to leave. I didn't know I could ask."

I didn't answer any of Zaara's questions on the ride home, texting Kiera over and over again without a reply.

"Back so soon?" Mom asked.

"I'm not feeling great."

Not a complete lie.

Not the first party I had come home early from.

Mom knew coming home sick didn't mean I was actually sick. "Dad and Imran probably haven't gotten very far, if you want to join them." Imran went trick-or-treating with Dad because he didn't have any friends to go with. Apparently neither did I.

"I'm going to my room."

"When did you finally figure out what happened?"

"Not until the next day."

Mom was reading the paper at the kitchen table when I heard her phone ring. Sunday mornings usually meant phone calls from India.

"Why hello!" Mom said, bright and loud after she answered the phone.

Followed by:

"Oh."

"I see."

"I don't think so."

"I know Sammy. She would never."

"Well, that's up to you."

I waited for her to say something once she got off the phone, but she went back to her paper.

"What was that about, Mom?" I asked.

"Oh, Kiera's mom just being Kiera's mom."

I wanted to ask more, but didn't want to admit I had been asked to leave her house.

"Kiera is always welcome to hang out here, but how about you don't go over there for a little while?" Mom said, trying to sound light and breezy, even though her knuckles turned white from holding the paper too tightly.

I played every possible scenario in my head, turned over every possible explanation, and when my phone finally rang with a call from Kiera, I ran upstairs and closed the door behind me.

"What happened last night?" I asked. I had studied every detail of the photos she posted, but there was not a single clue in the fireside s'mores or the duck-face selfies.

"The party was tons of fun," she yawned. My body had been tense and taut all night. Her yawn made me angry.

"Your mom kicked me out of your house, Kiera."

She giggled. Actually giggled. "Oh yeah, sorry about that." Like she had accidentally stepped on my foot.

"But what happened?" I asked again, almost pleading.

"My mom found the beers in the basement." She tilted her head like what she was saying was cute or funny. "I told her I had no idea how they got there, that you must have put them there."

She giggled again. I wanted to throw up.

"WHAT?" I asked, my anger intensified by her yawning, giggling, head-tilting casualness. "You said I snuck beer down to your basement?" Every part of this was hard for me to believe.

She looked over her shoulder. "Listen, I'm not even supposed to be speaking to you. That's my punishment for letting you talk me into this." Like that was now the truth. Like she was doing me a favor by calling. "I'd better go."

She disconnected before I said bye.

"And her mom believed her?" Alice asked. "Just like that?"

"Yup." I nodded.

"Harsh. I can't believe Kiera tried to pin the whole thing on you!" Alice said.

"She said it wasn't my type of party anyway. That she thought I'd understand."

"Brutal," Alice said.

Kiera's pool, Umma's dinner, The Halloween Incident. Three parties. Alice had used the word *brutal* to describe all three. She wasn't wrong.

54

Control or Be Controlled

I knew where Pete liked his extra guitar picks, how Noor liked her cymbals set up, and when the amp screeched, I showed Alice how to make the noise stop.

"How do you know all that?" Alice looked at me like I had pulled a coin out of her ear or made myself levitate.

"Now you know it too," I said.

"Nice T-shirt," Pete said, already unloading his stuff. "Hope you can live up to the title."

"Live up to what?" Leroy said, stepping on his dad's feet on his way out of the van, just like last time.

Billy sighed, rubbing his foot. "Say sorry, Leroy."

Leroy didn't strike me as the kind to apologize. I was right.

"Where's ImRAN?" he asked, pronouncing his name like my brother was in a race.

I was supposed to call him if Leroy was there. "He couldn't come," I lied to protect him.

"Oh, man," Leroy said, punching his own hand. That could have been my brother.

Noor was in bright, fiery red, from the bandanna in her hair to the color on her lips to the tennis shoes with the wedge heels.

"Whoa," Alice said. Her go-to phrase any time she couldn't find the right words. It happened more than you'd expect. "Your. Hair. Is. Amazing." Noor's hair was unleashed from last night's turban and in full, towering, gravity-defying glory of curls and volume.

"Sometimes it is," Noor said. "And sometimes it's a nightmare. A curly girl knows."

I pulled at my braid. "My hair is curly." The last time I didn't have it tied in a tight braid was kindergarten picture day. "But not that kind of curly."

Noor paused with a big blue box in her hands. "Well, what kind, then?"

I thought of that school picture still on the fridge. From the top of my head I drew a triangle out and back to my chin with the flats of my hands, like a pyramid was growing out of my neck.

"That's all about the product," Noor said. "I can show you after practice if you're interested."

Alice answered for me before I had a chance to say no. "Of course she's interested!"

I tugged at the comfort of my braid.

"By the way," Noor said, "we were talking on the way over here and wondering if you would make a video of the band. It's probably time to get a real gig, and a video might help."

A little bit of the heaviness I'd been carrying around since last night lifted. A tiny bit, but it was a start. "I'd love to!"

We closed and latched two of the metal boxes to use as seats while they tuned their instruments. I saw a text from Kiera come through on Alice's phone and she swiped to ignore it.

Mrs. Richardson popped her head out before the first song started, trying to talk over the jumble of guitar and drums. "Umma's not joining?" she asked, emphasizing the *ah* instead of the *Umm*, but I didn't try to correct her. Some words were hard to pronounce the right way no matter how much people tried.

"It was a great party last night," she said, pausing to gather her thoughts. "I hope Umma wasn't too upset."

I saw Alice swipe past another text.

Of course Umma was upset. I had upset her.

Everyone probably hated me for it. I hated myself.

"I'm such a klutz. I knew that tablecloth is special to your family and I still managed to spill all that red gravy. I hope those stains come out."

Reliving an embarrassing moment was my specialty. "Umma would never be upset about that, Mrs. Richardson. She always says, 'things are just things.'" Unfortunately, I was the one who knew exactly how to upset her. Pete ran back to the van to get another guitar pedal, and the quiet gave me room to speak. "If she can't get the stain out of the tablecloth, she will cut it into napkins and love the napkins. She's done that before."

Mrs. Richardson seemed relieved, smiling genuinely before returning inside, not interested in the band if there was no Umma to keep her company.

They started their first song; I couldn't recognize the tune. I focused on Noor's face through my camera. "Are they any good?" Alice asked, and I shrugged. I had no idea anymore.

When they were done, before cords were wrapped and boxes filled again, Noor was on her feet. "Hey, can you guys load up the van?" she said to the rest of the band. "I wanted to mess around with Samira's hair a little."

Leroy had stayed glued to his phone the entire time the band played, and Billy was pleading with him to turn it off. I didn't know if he was irritated with Leroy, or me, or both. "We're not paying her to get her hair done. She's the roadie. It says so right on her shirt."

"So does that make you Taco King?" Noor asked, pointing at his shirt. "And we're not paying her a thing."

"Fine. But we can't wait too long."

"Did I ask you to wait long?" Noor shot back.

Hair and makeup was Alice's thing. She was already hovering over my shoulder, practically salivating. "Can I record?" she asked.

"Umm, yeah," Noor replied, "especially if that means you'll give us a little room." That sort of comment didn't bother Alice one bit. I would have needed a hospital bed and an IV.

Noor rolled the hair tie down and untwined my braid. "I only have the basics on me, but we can do more another time if you'd like."

She soaked my hair with a squirt bottle before squeezing conditioner into her palm and rubbing her hands together. "Sometimes work runs late and I need a little refresher." I never thought of their lives outside the band. "I have a few supplies with me all the time."

She divided my hair into smaller sections and spread the conditioner from root to tips, talking the whole time.

"Us curly-haired girls are different. We have to treat

our hair with the respect it deserves. It's a control-or-be-controlled sort of situation." She lifted a strand of Alice's red hair before letting it drop again. "Her hair doesn't turn into an evil beast if you treat it badly. I'm not going to say that's lucky. But I will say it's easier."

She finished combing my hair with her fingers before twirling small sections until the curl sprung up. "Rules are different for us. Use a brush, and instead of taming, our hair goes wild."

Noor kept twirling. Sometimes using one index finger. Sometimes two.

"Moisture, moisture, moisture. We're like a camel in the middle of a desert. We can never get enough."

She orbited around me, and Alice followed her to catch the best angles. Like they were moons and I was the sun.

"I think the daily struggle with our hair makes us stronger." She revolved around me, twirling here, scrunching there, finally rocking so far back on her heels I feared she would fall over. "So when someone says or does something we don't like, we don't get upset. We've already used up our worry on our hair. We have no more for you, you know?"

I had no idea what she was talking about.

"The last thing to remember is that once you're done, you're done. The more you touch your hair, the more likely you turn into a frizz ball."

Noor stepped back to admire her work. "Like me. Mess around too much with me and I'm not going to be happy."

She took out a tiny mirror from her handbag to let me see. "And voila, meet your new hair, Samira."

I could see bits of my curls in the tiny mirror, like perfect coiled springs. I pulled one, stretching it out, letting it go.

"Ahem," Noor said. "I literally just said not to touch, didn't I?"

The van honked twice. "Okay, I've got to go. You look strong and beautiful with the mane of a lion." She threw her equipment in her bag and was off.

My head felt lighter without the tight braid pulling me down, but I felt exposed. I was glad to not have a bigger mirror.

"You want to see the video?" Alice asked, holding her phone to my face.

"I'm not sure," I answered, feeling the edges of the hair, the curliness, the smoothness, ignoring the last of many commandments Noor had thrown my way.

I couldn't interpret Alice's expression. Did I look ridiculous? Look-at-me hair seemed like the kind of thing Noor could pull off. Not me.

I let the video play, cringing a little, squinting my eyes to blur the picture like I did when I watched a scary movie, or saw my favorite tree wrapped in toilet paper.

"You look amazing," Alice said.

I do?

I scrubbed through the video to get to the final product.

I kind of did.

55

Two Birds, One Stone

"Sammy," Imran said when I walked in, "your hair is all over the place."

Imran never colored inside the lines or followed directions to build his Lego creations. Being all over the place was his thing. I knew he was trying to pay me a compliment.

"Thanks, Imran."

"Wow!" Umma said, trying out the word. "You look great, Samira. You like it?"

My hair bounced with every step. "Noor showed me how. I think . . . I love it!" I answered truthfully, still not able to look her in the eye. Embarrassed by the kindness I didn't deserve.

The outline of my image on the microwave door was rounder, my reflection on the surface of the toaster looked so different, and my hair didn't fit in the mirror where we hung keys. Like there was a stranger in my kitchen.

My phone rang with a call from Zaara.

"Sammy? Oh my goodness! You look fabulous," she said. "Turn around so I can see the back. Mom, Dad, come see Sammy's hair!"

The three of them crowded around the phone, the picture freezing and unfreezing, the voices not in time with the movement of mouths. "Gorgeous," Dad's voice said, even though Mom's mouth was open.

"Beautiful," Mom's voice said, even though Zaara looked like she was speaking.

There were garbled questions about how and why and when. I tried to explain Noor, but they didn't even know about Pete's band. So much had happened since they left.

"How's dance practice going, Zaara?" I asked, when Mom and Dad were off-screen.

"Terrible," she replied. "Horrible."

I wanted to tell her about the video of Kiera and me at the party, about hurting Umma's feelings, but the catch in her voice, the way her excitement dropped so quickly, made me stop. I wished I hadn't brought up the dance. "Why don't you tell them you don't want to?"

She chewed on a piece of hair. That was a new one for her. "Before you lose all your hair."

"You don't get it." Her eyes flickered to the door. "I always do what they want. I can't be difficult for them. I can't because—" And she stopped mid-sentence.

"Because Imran is difficult?" I asked. I knew what she meant. She nodded sharply, too quickly and too many times. "Because I'm difficult?" I asked slowly. I had never thought of myself as difficult.

"You're not difficult, Sammy. But I don't want them to have to worry about me."

"Because they're too busy worrying about me and Imran." I said the words like a statement even though I was asking her a question.

She picked up the end of her hair again. "It's not that they're worried about you. They're just concerned you don't always stand up for yourself."

"That's why Mom always puts me in those clubs?" I asked. The thought had never occurred to me before.

"Well, why did *you* think she made you join?"

"I don't know," I answered. "Torture?"

I got Zaara to smile. Like a real smile. "Well, two birds with one stone."

56

Umma Always Knows

I carried Zaara's words around the rest of the day. I knew Mom and Dad worried about me, about whether I ate my vegetables, made my bed, scrubbed behind my ears.

I never thought they worried about me like they worry about Imran.

I never knew Zaara had to protect them from me.

Which was why she had to be in the dance even when she didn't want to.

Basically, I was the one forcing Zaara to dance.

Umma had her legs tucked under her on the couch. "Umma," I called quietly, sitting next to her.

"Yes, molay." She set aside the magazine she was reading, the squiggles of Malayalam like Greek to me, the little comic with a woman waving her rolling pin at a mob totally undecipherable.

"I'm so sorry." I started to cry even though she was the one with the hurt feelings. Not quiet, pretty sniffles, but big, blubbering, snot-filled tears. "I don't know why I said those things. I hope you can make napkins out of the tablecloth I ruined." I knew the words would make no sense to her. Umma pulled me in so my apology muffled against her. "I didn't mean it at all. Not one bit." She pressed her lips against my head and squeezed me tight. "I'm so happy you're here. I don't know why I said any of that."

She pushed me back by my shoulders for a moment so I could see her eyes, tipping my chin up until I looked at her.

"You don't have to apologize, molay. I know already."

And she pulled me back in so I could finish sobbing, until I could breathe again.

57

Excited and Happy Are Not the Same Thing

"We're trending!" Alice shouted as soon as I answered the phone, before I could say hi.

"Who is?"

"You!"

"*Me?* How?"

She sent me the link to the video of Noor doing my hair, and there were over five thousand views and hundreds of comments. So, not trending, technically, but that was still a lot of people.

Umma looked over my shoulder and took a few chips from my bowl. "What's all the noise?" she asked, reaching for the bottle of mango pickle that was never more than an arm's length away.

I showed her the post and the views and the counter ticking up.

"All those people watch your video? And they like?"

I nodded my head. "They all watched the video. Most of them like it."

She scrolled through the comments, adding a dab of spicy pickle to her chip before taking a bite. "People you don't know—this makes you happy?"

"Well, it's exciting. My video might go viral, Umma!"

She kept scrolling up, pausing, zooming in, pinching the screen back to size. "And this makes you happy?" she asked again, because I hadn't answered her question the first time.

"It's what everyone wants." She looked over her glasses, forcing me to answer her question. "Yes, it makes me happy."

And it did.

Until it didn't.

58

Cleaning up the Front Step ... Again

I woke up the next morning with the impression of my phone pressed into my cheek. We had over ten thousand likes and hundreds of comments. Some liked my hair, some didn't. Some liked my necklace, some didn't. Some liked my parents, some didn't. Which didn't even make sense, since my parents had nothing to do with anything.

I texted Alice but got no reply, which was unusual for Alice. I decided to show up at her house uninvited, which was unusual for me. The mere idea shifted the balance of my universe, knocking over my glass, spilling orange juice all over the counter, dripping down to the floor. At least that's who I blamed for this—the universe. I wiped the mess, but my sock still stuck to the spot like Velcro.

I bent to wipe it again and hit my head on the edge of the cabinet. I should have left it sticky.

An ambulance passed me on the road. I had never seen one leave our neighborhood, and even without the flashing lights, my feet and heartbeat sped up.

A small crowd was gathered outside Alice's house. Kiera and her mom were there, talking to a lady who Alice was leaning against. The woman wore her blond hair piled high, a bright yellow leather jacket with matching pants, and black heels that came to a skinny pointy end, giving her the look of a No. 2 pencil. Kiera's mother pulled her pearls away from her neck with her red manicured nail. There was a sense of worry—in the tight circle they formed, the downturn of their lips, the whispers in which they spoke.

The smell of egg hung in the air. Not eggs that smelled like vanilla, mixed for cake batter. This smell made my stomach turn, as did the looks on everyone's faces.

"Umm . . . what happened?" An ambulance. Kiera's mom's worry pearls. The smell of eggs. I couldn't put the pieces together into one story.

"Our house was egged," Alice answered, rubbing her arm with one hand, then switching, trying to keep the cold away on this warm morning.

"What?"

"Someone threw eggs at our house," Alice repeated, explaining the part I didn't need explained.

"When?"

"This morning sometime. It was there when we woke up."

"Who?" Apparently I could only speak in one-word questions.

"We were discussing that," Kiera's mom said.

Alice spoke to the No. 2 pencil. "Mom, this is Samira."

"Oh Samira how wonderful to meet you I've been meaning to come around and say hello but with all the unpacking and moving and clients and oh everything else I haven't had a chance I'm so glad Alice found a friend so quickly and oh I love the hair and the video and maybe when I'm working a curly-hair client I'll need to call on you and oh my goodness is that the time I'd better get to the hospital so Mom isn't in the ER all by herself," she said in one big breath, before she wiggled her fingers and ran off, getting into her car, leaving behind a cloud of perfume soured by the smell of egg.

"Bye, Mom, let me know how Grandma is doing," Alice said, her eyes puffy, her voice shaky.

Her mom rolled down the window as she drove slowly past us. "I'll call you as soon as I see her, sweetie. Don't worry, I'm sure she will be fine."

Like her mom, Kiera pulled at her necklace when she worried. She was wearing the Bean pendant I bought both of us when my family went to Chicago. She had not worn that necklace for a few years and quickly tucked it under her shirt when I noticed. "There were a lot of comments about your necklace on the video yesterday. I forgot how pretty it was."

Kiera left with her mother. The small crowd dispersed, patting Alice on the shoulder, offering prayers and wishes and breakfast before they left.

"What was with the ambulance? What happened to your grandmother?" I couldn't imagine what I would do if something happened to Umma. I hoped I would never have to find out.

"The paramedics thought she may have broken her hip," Alice said, pulling at the edges of her pajamas, biting her lower lip. I bit my lip when I wanted to stop myself from crying.

"I'm so sorry, Alice. What happened?" Umma was always telling Imran to pick up his toys so she didn't trip over them and break a hip. I thought that was just a thing she said, but maybe that's how hips were broken.

"The egging," Alice replied. I still couldn't put the two things together.

I didn't want to push Alice if she didn't want to speak.

"The eggs made her fall?" I still asked.

"Grandma never sleeps past three a.m." The two of us stood side by side, which is a weird position when you're talking to each other. "She heard noises early in the morning and stepped outside. I wish she hadn't, but Grandma does what she wants to do." I knew that type of grandma. "She missed a step and fell down. She couldn't get up. She was stuck out here for hours." Her voice was hoarse. "While we slept comfortably in our beds."

I looked away so I wouldn't see her cry. I didn't like people looking at me when I cried. "Is she going to be okay?"

"I think so," she said, and then corrected herself. "I hope so. I'm so glad Kiera and her mom were driving by. They're the ones who found her."

The thought of Umma lying outside by herself, not able to get any of us for help, made me want to cry too.

"Hey, why don't we clean up the mess?" I remembered that sense of relief when the toilet paper was gone.

There were more than a dozen eggs smashed all over the front door, dripping down the doorknob, crushed into the doormat. Cleaning off a front step was how we hung out the first time. Alice was quiet and focused, the sound of scrubbing brushes replacing conversation.

Who knew egg would be so hard to get out? Who knew that toilet paper could seem to hang around even after it was gone?

"Is it okay if we don't hang out?" Alice asked. "I think I want to be alone."

"Sure. I get it." I totally did. "Just text me when you're ready."

Daal and Eggs

I tried to keep myself busy, keep myself distracted. The submission date for the contest was only five days away. I stopped fiddling with my first two videos, like Mrs. Markley suggested. The third video was supposed to be about "My World," and I didn't even know what that meant.

I waited for Alice to call me, giving her space to recover, checking my phone all day, even waking up in the middle of the night to see if she had texted.

"Oh, Samira," Umma said, when I came down for breakfast, bleary-eyed. She fluffed my hair from the bottom. "I got off the phone with Dana. Alice's grandmother will be home in few days. She didn't break her hip."

"So she's okay?" I asked, not quite understanding why

she still needed a few days in the hospital.

Umma moved pots from cupboard to stove. "Inshah Allah, she will be. Let's make some food and drop to Alice's family, okay?"

She made rice and daal and chicken curry. Comfort food. I couldn't convince Umma that our comfort food might not be their comfort food. "Silly. Everyone loves daal."

I hate daal.

Imran and I carefully pulled the wagon with covered plates of comfort-not-comfort food to Alice's, and I hoped she would ask me to stay.

"Gross, what's that smell?" Imran asked as we neared their front porch. Our attempted scrubbing had only made things worse, and the bottom of my foot stuck to poorly-cleaned surfaces for the second time in two days.

"Samira," Alice's mom said, still wearing her head-to-toe yellow outfit, the exact color of egg yolks.

"My grandmother made you food. She tried to make it less spicy, but that doesn't always work," I said, handing her the first plate, giving her fair warning. I looked behind her, hoping to see Alice.

"Well, it smells delicious," she said, her voice tired, without the peppiness of the day before. "Please tell her thank you from me."

Imran balanced a plate in each hand even though I

had asked him not to. I didn't need to be cleaning up one more mess.

Boxes, opened and unopened, cluttered the front entrance. I held another dish in front of me for Alice's mom, not finding a cleared surface to set it down. "Is Alice home?" Imran asked.

She gestured for us to follow her into the kitchen. "She's taking a nap. All the worry wore her out." There were stacks of books on the floor, half-finished puzzles on the kitchen table, a green velvet couch with mismatched couch cushions. Imran made a beeline for the table; he had a hard time leaving a puzzle not completed. I liked how Alice's house felt messy and cozy.

I helped put the dishes we brought into the fridge, moving things around to make space.

"All the neighbors have been dropping off food," she said. "Everyone has been so kind."

Not everyone. I mean, someone must have thrown those eggs. I didn't point that out to her, and was grateful the thought didn't occur to Imran.

An Accusation but Also a Decision

Imran pulled the empty wagon back easily. "Hey, Kiera," he shouted, waving into the distance. Ha ha. Imran is such a joker. Except, of course, he didn't know how to make jokes like that, didn't know that bumping into Kiera would be a bad joke.

She had both hands wrapped around a loaf pan. "I'm surprised to see you here," Kiera said to me, ignoring Imran's greeting.

"Is that banana bread?" he asked, totally oblivious to the tension between Kiera and me.

"Why would my being here surprise you?" I asked. I was friends with Alice too.

"How come you don't bring banana bread to our house anymore?" Imran asked. Half my life was spent praying Imran would stop talking.

"She knows you were the one," Kiera said to me. "Everyone does."

"How come you don't come over anymore?" Imran asked, not at all bothered that she hadn't even acknowledged his presence.

"The one?" I asked, confused by the overlapping conversations.

She scrunched her face and pinched her nose at the smell. "The one who egged Alice's house."

"What are you talking about? I didn't egg Alice's house." I would never.

"I saw you," she said, walking to the front door, not allowing the bombshell she'd just delivered to slow her down.

Imran jumped in front of her, playfully pretending to reach for her banana bread. They used to have that kind of relationship. But not anymore. I pulled him away.

"You saw me egg Alice's house?" I asked, not yet understanding the accusation.

Kiera twisted her mouth in thought. "Well, I saw you leaving her house in the morning, carrying a bag. We told Alice's mother already."

My head was swirling. Alice and her mom thought I egged their house. That I made her grandmother fall?

"I bet Alice hasn't been answering your calls and said she didn't want to see you, right?" she asked.

She was right. That had happened.

"I guess you and Alice won't be hanging out anymore.

No more cute videos." She opened her eyes super wide and pretended to twirl bits of her hair, mimicking our last video.

Like so many times before, Kiera left me speechless.

"Next time," Imran yelled as I squeezed his arm too hard, "maybe next time you can meet my new best friend."

I would give anything for there to not be a next time.

"Can I ask you something, Umma?" I had replayed Kiera's conversation all the way home, and it still made no sense. The TV blared at the earsplitting volume Umma preferred. We tried our best to not bother her during the thirty minutes her show lasted. I weighed whether this counted as an emergency or not. "After the show is fine."

She patted the seat next to her, and I sat down. "Of course. You sure you can wait until show is over?"

The weight of Umma on the couch slid me toward her. I didn't mind.

The actress on TV kept her finger up the whole time she monologued, her eyes bloodshot, her tears big and fat. Umma was watching her favorite Malayalam soap opera. Even without subtitles, I could follow the story. The hand gestures and over-expressive eyebrows gave away every emotion.

"She's telling him she's not going to take his—how you say it—his crap anymore," Umma explained, not turning to me when she talked, not blinking so she wouldn't miss a second. The woman picked up her suitcase, which must have been empty judging from the way she lifted it, and got in the back seat of her car so the driver could whisk her away.

Umma unwrapped her arm from around me to clap twice in excitement. "I've been waiting for her to do that since first episode."

"How many episodes have there been?" I asked as the credits rolled up the screen.

She thought for a moment, drawing invisible tally marks in the air. "Three years. I've been wanting her to leave for three years!" She laughed at her own silliness. "Now, what did you want to talk about, Samira?"

I wasn't exactly sure.

"It feels like everyone is mad at me," I said without emotion, like I was stating facts unrelated to me. "Alice. Probably her mom. Probably her grandmother."

"How could everyone be mad at you? You're like me, Sam—"

I stopped her from finishing because I didn't want to hear the lie. "I'm not anything like you, Umma. Nothing." I tucked my legs under me and pressed myself deeper into her. "You make us feel good about ourselves.

I don't do that. Everyone loves you. No one likes me. You have friends wherever you go. I have none."

Umma turned off the TV, cutting short the Indian ads for drinks and snacks not available at our grocery store. I didn't have to ask Traci-Mary to know.

"You are so much like me, Samira, because we are happiest when we are helping others." I didn't see it, not at all. I never helped anyone. Not even myself. Especially not myself. "Tell me what's bothering you," she said.

I didn't know where to start. "Alice thinks I egged her house." I spread out the end of her saree over my legs, pulling at the edges.

"Why would she think that, molay?" Umma asked. "Did you tell Alice it wasn't you?" She shifted in her seat to release the rest of the saree pallu so I would have more to fidget with.

"I couldn't tell her, Umma. She's not answering my calls. She didn't come downstairs."

"Why would she think you did egging, Samira?"

I rested my head on her shoulder. "Kiera told them she saw me leaving their house that morning. I wasn't even there, Umma."

She patted my head. "Kiera is not a good friend." It was the meanest thing I'd ever heard Umma say about anyone.

"I shouldn't have let her get away with the toilet papering," I said.

"Why do you say that?" Umma asked.

"If I told her that I knew she toilet papered my tree, if I stood up for myself, maybe she wouldn't keep doing this to me." My thoughts went back to the Halloween party.

"Who do you think it was, Samira?" Umma asked, holding her arms out in front of her, waiting for me to help her off the couch. "Who do you think throwing eggs on Alice's house?"

I pulled her up, the top of Umma's head at eye level.

"I think it was Kiera," I answered, "but I don't know for sure. What I do know for sure is that I don't want Alice to think I egged her house," I said.

Little crinkles appeared around Umma's eyes and between her eyebrows. "Why?"

"Why? Because Alice is my friend, Umma."

"And?" She leaned closer, pulling my head toward her.

"And I finally have a real friend." There, I said it out loud. "Had a real friend," I corrected myself.

"Last question, Samira. You want to do something about this or not?" She pressed our foreheads together.

"I do," I answered, enjoying the warmth from her forehead.

"Then you do something like this." She snapped her

fingers. "No more crap," Umma said.

"No more crap," I repeated.

I wished I had a suitcase to pick up so I could exit dramatically.

61

Stranger Danger

The next morning I came downstairs ready to go. But deciding to take action is very different from actually taking action.

"Umma, have you seen my notebook? The one with the green stripes on it?" I asked, slamming cupboards and drawers. I had no use for a notebook. "Have you seen the blue flashlight?" The sun was in the middle of the sky. There was no need for flashlights. When I crisscrossed the living room for the third time looking desperately for a pink highlighter, Umma stepped in.

"How about new doorbell camera? Maybe something helpful there?"

I liked the idea because it was simple and loved the idea because I wouldn't have to leave the house to gather information. I forwarded through video footage on my laptop, Umma peering over my shoulder.

"Whose blue car is that?" she asked. A newspaper flew out the window, missing our driveway completely. Mom's perpetual complaint.

"Newspaper delivery," I told her.

The ambulance on its way to Alice's house triggered the camera next. The time stamp on the video meant I would be leaving the house soon too. I watched myself walking to Alice's house, curls bouncing, blissfully unaware of how things were going to change that day.

"Oh, there's you, Samira. You look hungry," Umma said. All you could see was the back of my head. I tripped over the crack on the first step, but steadied myself so I didn't fall. Real-me cheered for video-me. I wrote down the time in my notebook.

"Write down time of ambulance too," Umma said, tapping the next line in the notebook. "See, this is proof. You don't even leave house in the morning."

I thought about the Halloween party and the toilet papering. "But it doesn't prove Kiera was the one." This time I needed that.

Umma put a bowl of my favorite Kerala mixture in front of me. "Eat. You looked hungry." A day ago, the back of my head did.

"Maybe the newspaper delivery people saw something

suspicious. Alice's grandmother must have already been outside when they passed by." Umma didn't read the local paper, but we kept getting them. "Can you call and ask them, Umma?"

"I cannot, Samira. No one understand anything I say on phone," Umma said, putting a bowl of nuts next to the mixture I hadn't touched yet.

I had never called a grown-up before, definitely not a grown-up stranger. This was exactly what I had been taught to not do my entire life. I found the number in the survival binder, and let the phone ring, hoping no one would answer.

"Yeah?" a gruff voice shouted from the other end of the phone.

I must have dialed the wrong number.

"Umm, do I have the wrong number?" I asked, the back of my neck getting hot. That's where the sweat always starts.

"Well, how the heck am I supposed to know that?"

He had a point.

"I'm looking for the person who delivers our newspaper," I said, and gave him our address.

A car door dinged. "If you have a missing paper, use the website. We'll get to your concerns right away."

I knew from Mom's complaining that they would, in

fact, not get to our concerns right away. I had the right number.

"I don't have a complaint," I said, before he could hang up on me. "I had a question for the person who delivered our paper." I wasn't sure if he had hung up. "Hello?"

I heard his car start. "My son, Brian, delivers the local newspaper for your neighborhood."

Ah, his son. No wonder the delivery person never got fired.

"Hey, Brian, someone wants to talk to you about your route." The phone crackled and I imagined it being passed to Brian as I listened in on their conversation.

"Dad, I swear I delivered every paper on time. Every one."

"Sure you did. Then just talk to the lady and let her know."

Lady? That was my cue, I guess.

"Hi," I said. "I was wondering if you saw anything strange when you delivered our paper yesterday?" I repeated our address.

Brian was eating the world's loudest potato chips as he spoke. "Your house is the one toilet papered last week, right? Wow, they really did a number on you guys."

At least we were memorable. Comes in handy for these situations.

"Yeah." He didn't need to know my ex–best friend did it. Brian wasn't the kind to care. "A house down the street from ours got egged yesterday morning. I was wondering if you saw anything suspicious."

His voice was faint through the chip chomping. "Wow, it's always the neighborhoods that look the quietest that are wild. But no, I didn't see anything egged."

"You're sure? It was the house where the road curves."

Crunch, crunch. "Absolutely. I would remember, because I almost ran over that girl on the side of the road."

"A girl?" I asked. A kid on the side of the road at five a.m. didn't seem suspicious to Brian? "What did she look like?"

But Brian and his dad were at it again. *"You almost ran someone over. I've told you a million times, you can't drive with your headphones on. I bet you were wearing your headphones, weren't you?"*

"I swear, Dad, I wasn't."

The line went dead.

If the girl he saw secretly enjoyed Hindi movies and also knew how to throw a roll of toilet paper, then my suspicions were correct.

Phew . . . I Didn't Have It in Me

I now had two pieces of information: 1. My video doorbell proved I didn't leave the house until after the ambulance, and 2. There was another girl.

"Go ask others. Maybe they see something," Umma said as she tied the newspapers together for recycling.

"Who's standing outside at five a.m. looking for clues?" I helped her lift the bundles.

"Oh, this whole neighborhood full of old people. Old people always awake at five a.m."

She expected me to go knocking on doors, asking questions? I wished Alice were with me. Every time Alice had oohed and aahed about the way I'd figured things out, not once did I ooh and aah about the way she made it possible. Without Alice, I would never have sat in Mrs. Richardson's house uninvited; she forced me out of my room; she made me think about who toilet papered my tree when I preferred to pretend none of it ever happened.

I mustered every bit of Alice I had in me, and every speck of Umma I resembled. I would start with Mrs. Richardson, where I was comfortable. Sure, that wasn't lion-tamer brave, but it was something.

Mrs. Richardson opened the door, swirling a glass of lemonade so the ice clinked. "Samira, your hair. What an excellent surprise." She still scowled, but she sounded genuinely pleased. "Come in. I was catching up with Mr. Miller from next door. He just got back from his daughter's wedding." She waved me in.

Mr. Miller was wearing a green plaid shirt, his hair was neatly plastered to his head, and his smile was wide across his face. "Why, hello," he said. His voice was kind, but I had only prepared and planned to talk to one person, not two.

"Pete and the band will be here soon. Samira is their roadie," Mrs. Richardson explained, but I wasn't there for official roadie business.

"Umm, I was wondering if I could ask you about Alice's house being egged, about whether you saw anything unusual yesterday morning," I said.

"We were just talking about that," Mr. Miller said. "I'm so glad her grandmother wasn't seriously hurt."

I found a seat close enough that I wouldn't have to yell from across the room, but far enough so they couldn't see me sweat. "Umm, there's a rumor going around, uh, that I egged Alice's house." I tried not to move, so the chair wouldn't creak.

"Someone did mention your name," Mrs. Richardson said, "but I didn't believe it for a second." She turned her attention to Mr. Miller. "Remember when these girls used to pull weeds for us? Some people only pull off the heads, but Samira always got them by their roots. Someone who pulls weeds out by the roots could never do something like that."

Mr. Miller nodded seriously. I didn't understand what she meant, but the logic seemed to be in my favor so I didn't question it.

"I wanted to help Alice figure out who egged her house." Alice would do the same for me. In fact, she had.

Mrs. Richardson took a sip of her lemonade. My mouth was really dry, and I wished she'd offer me a glass. "Sorry, Samira, I didn't see anything until I heard the commotion from the ambulance."

Mr. Miller nodded along. "And I got here from the airport after all the excitement, so I'm not much help."

Doors slammed outside. "Pete must be here," Mrs. Richardson said.

I stood up, grateful for an excuse to leave. "I'd better

go help them unload their stuff."

Mrs. Richardson directed her attention back to Mr. Miller. "Wait until you hear Pete's band; they've gotten really good." I wasn't sure if I agreed with her, but that's exactly the kind of thing Umma would say about me.

"Hair's looking fierce," Noor said, and I reached for my curls before pulling my hand away.

Pete's guitar hung from his neck while he unloaded his pedalboard. He never let anyone touch his guitar because it was too important to him. He never let anyone touch his pedalboard because it was on the verge of completely falling apart. Anything else, I could help with. "So, are you going to start setting up, or are we going to hang around talking about hair all day?"

I hoped they hadn't heard about Alice's house, about me being the prime suspect.

"Any news on how your friend's grandmother is doing?" Noor asked. "Mrs. Richardson called when we were driving over, to warn us about the smell."

"She's going to be okay," I said, setting up the mic stand. "She's supposed to come back from the hospital in a couple days."

"That's a relief," Noor said. "Especially because we heard you were the one who egged her house." Her eyebrows were knitted in concern, her voice somber.

I shifted my weight from one foot to the other. I

should have stayed inside with Mrs. Richardson. She might have even offered me a glass of lemonade by now. Probably not, but maybe.

Noor covered her mouth in mock horror. The three of them broke into loud, knee-slapping, hold-your-tummy laughter.

"Funniest thing we've heard in a while. You don't have it in you, girlie," Billy said.

Didn't have what in me?

"Me? I was the kind of kid who would do something dumb like that," Pete said. "Not you."

It felt like a compliment.

I was afraid Alice wouldn't find the accusation funny, didn't know what "kind of kid" I was, that I didn't have it in me, that I pulled weeds by the roots.

Problem-Solver Extraordinaire

Without Alice by my side, I wondered how many doors I would have the energy to knock on. Turns out the answer was one.

I called Zaara. She had her sheets pulled above her nose so all I could see was her hair in knots around her and her eyes sparkling with a smile.

"I hope I didn't wake you up," I said, shimmying my shoulders to get deeper in the beanbag. "I know it's super early, but I thought you'd be up practicing. Isn't the wedding tonight?" I would have been curled up in a ball. Zaara had probably practiced to perfection. Her solution to worry was the opposite of mine.

"Yup," Zaara said, beaming.

"And are you ready? Moves all mastered?" I asked, shaking my head from side to side like they did in Bollywood movies.

"Even better," Zaara said. "I'm not dancing."

I tried to sit up straight to show my surprise, but a beanbag isn't built for surprise moves. "You're not?"

"Nope." She shook her head to emphasize. "And it's all thanks to you."

I tried again to sit up straight. "Me?"

She nodded. "I don't know what you said to Mom and Dad." I didn't remember saying anything. "They asked me if I really wanted to do the dance or not. At first I said yes, like I always do. They kept asking, and you won't believe it, Sammy." She leaned closer to me through the phone. "I told them I didn't want to be in the dance."

I didn't understand the big deal. I told them I didn't want to do things all the time and it never seemed to matter.

"You are the best problem solver, Sammy. The best."

I didn't see it.

64

Snowballs in Summer

I'm a problem solver, I reminded myself on my way to the house I had been avoiding, taking the long way because problems solvers didn't need to be in a rush to get there.

I pulled my shoulders back and held my head high at the door. Ten. I'd count to ten for someone to open the door at Kiera's grandparents' house. Ten seemed like a brave number. They probably hadn't seen or heard anything anyway. Seven. Seven was a brave-enough number. Like they were going to rat out their granddaughter? It was never going to happen. Five. Five was good enough.

I rang the bell. Last year I would have let myself in.

"You have to pull harder," I heard Kiera say, "the door's sticky." It had been for years. "Here, let me." There was jostling and shuffling on the other side before Kiera pulled open the door. All smirk and head tilt.

"Sammy, it's you." I recognized the other three from push-ups in my front yard and the backyard pool party and noses eventually pierced. Towels were draped over their shoulders, not a red onesie in sight. Their group was lesser for it. "We were going for a swim."

Obviously. "Umm, yeah," I said. I wasn't an idiot, even when I sounded like one.

"Alice should be here soon," Kiera added, "but I'm guessing you aren't here to swim. You don't have your onesie on."

Push-up guy laughed like a honking duck. "Dude, I heard you egged someone's house and killed an old lady or something. So not cool." Without his mustache, I actually wasn't 100 percent sure he was push-up guy.

"No one died," I said, although I felt like I might. "And it wasn't me." My shoulders hurt from holding them pulled back for so long.

"Sure it wasn't." Kiera adjusted the towel on her shoulder. My towel. The one so faded you could only see Olaf throwing snowballs if you knew he was there. "What are you doing here anyway, Sammy?"

I crossed my arms tight against my body. Like a hug, because I needed one. "I wanted to ask your grandparents some questions in case they saw anything weird the morning Alice's house was egged."

She pushed her sunglasses down from the top of her head so I couldn't see her eyes. "Weird like what?"

"You know, someone sneaking out of the house at an odd hour? Missing any eggs from the fridge?" I squeezed my arms tighter until I almost couldn't breathe.

"Are we swimming or what?" asked the girl with the neon swimsuit, popsicle dripping down her arm.

Kiera rested her hand on her hip. "I don't know what you're trying to say, Sammy." She knew.

"I'm not trying to say anything, Kiera. I'm saying it. I didn't egg Alice's house. You did." I released the death grip I had on myself so I could take a full breath.

The other three hummed a low, long "ooooooooh." Like my big revelation, my accusation, was a joke to them.

Kiera stumbled over her words. She wasn't used to me talking to her like that. "Oh, oh. And I'm sure you have proof, right?"

"Yes, I have proof, and that's MY towel," I said, pulling Olaf off her shoulder, like the two had anything to do with each other.

"Oooooh," rumbled her friends, slapping each other's backs. "Busted."

"You've got proof?" Kiera asked, her voice squeaking higher.

"Oh, I've got proof," I said, my voice matching hers,

octave for octave. I did not have proof. Not a bit.

The oohs stopped mid-laugh. Amy with the nose ring swiveled on her heel. "Wait, really, Kiera? You egged her house? That's so not cool."

Used-to-have-a-mustache-guy also stopped laughing. "No one's supposed to get hurt. Plus, we would never use eggs, only toilet paper."

"Hold on. You guys toilet papered my house?" I asked. The thought of multiple people sneaking around my yard at night, toilet papering my tree stung even worse than if it were Kiera by herself. "You guys were in on it too? Was it just a stupid prank to you?" It was so much more to me.

"Wait—you never went back to explain?" Amy asked, turning her whole body to Kiera. "To clean up? Those were the rules, Kiera."

"Rules for what?" I asked. I deserved to know.

Neon-Swimsuit licked the bottom of her hand before the popsicle's sticky sweetness dripped to the floor. "Kiera was so desperate to be part of our friend group, we made up an initiation prank. We told her she'd have to toilet paper someone's house. We didn't think she would really do it."

Kiera's jaw gaped, like actually opened.

"You knew that, right?" Neon-Swimsuit said, focused

on catching another drip. "We all thought you were super annoying." She looked up to see Kiera with her mouth open. "What? We like you now."

"And we especially like your pool," Maybe-he's-the-mustache-guy said, smiling.

"But we'd never allow eggs," Amy with the nose ring said. "That's just mean. And way too much cleanup."

"Th-th-that doesn't even make sense," Kiera stammered. "Why would I even egg Alice's house? I like Alice."

As opposed to me.

I had been thinking about this ever since Alice and I scrubbed her front steps, and I had come up with the only reasoning that made any sense. "You egged her house so you could pin the whole thing on me. So that Alice wouldn't want to be friends with me anymore."

Kiera's friends made sounds of disbelief and offered grunts and words of disappointment.

But I had finally said what I wanted to say, what I needed to say.

65

The Beginning of an Idea

My flip-flops sounded like suction cups as I ran down Kiera's driveway. My feelings collided against each other. I slowed down past Alice's house. I had been brave enough for one day, and deserved to hide in my room like I had planned since the first day of summer. But I had taken the long way home from Kiera's for a reason. I knocked on the door and pressed the bell at the same time. I rang-knocked again when there was no answer, because being persistent was the kind of thing Alice would do.

"Answer the door, Alice," I yelled into the air, to no one at all. "Please."

The curtain moved a tiny bit.

"I'm going to stand here until you come out," I yelled again.

If the situation were reversed, Alice wouldn't just sit back. Doing nothing wasn't Alice's style.

"Maybe I'll yell," I said, already doing that, "or sing . . . or dance." In my desperation, I grouped together the most unlike-me things to do. "I know you're there, Alice." She was probably changing into her swimsuit to go to Kiera's.

Taking my threat to the next level, I scrolled down playlists, stopping at the Bollywood song I was named after. I increased the volume as high as possible and wiped my sweaty palms on Olaf's face.

"I'm starting to dance," I yelled to no one at all, waiting for her to stop me. This was worse than the nightmare where I was running down the school halls in my underwear, late for a test.

I put my hands in the air, jerking my shoulders up and down like I had seen in Hindi movies.

"Here I go." I wasn't sure if I was warning her, or myself, or the general universe.

I turned my hands like I was unscrewing lightbulbs. Or putting them back in. It was all very confusing.

"I'm doing it," I yelled again, unsure what the *it* referred to.

A sour taste rushed into the back of my throat. I always thought seeing me dance could induce nausea. I didn't expect to do it to myself.

Thankfully the song ended, but I wasn't sure whether to continue this display or call its time of death.

"Well, look who is finally letting loose and having fun!" Alice said. My body had never felt tighter, and I was most definitely not having fun.

I said the words quickly, letting them tumble out before I could change my mind, before she could change hers. "Alice, I did not egg your house. I would never. I need you to know that."

"You egging my house?" She put both her hands on her head. "You think I would believe that?" She pushed me gently. "No one did. Not for a second."

A classical piece was playing from my phone, full of drums and drama, one I had downloaded for a video of thunderclouds I had been editing for my video submission.

"Besides, I know who egged my house," she said. "It was Kiera." A cymbal crashed, jolting both of us into laughter at the ridiculous coincidence of the soundtrack. I turned the music off.

"You're not the only one with powers of deduction, Samira. I see things too." She pulled both eyes wider with her hands to show me. "Based on the pattern of the thrown eggs, I knew where the person stood." Wow. "The shells were stamped with the name of a local farm and not a grocery store." No way. "There was one footprint in the stickiness of the whites over there." Unbelievable. "I put all that together and came to my conclusion."

"Wow, Alice, that's amazing."

She nodded. "I know."

"And you were still going swimming with her?" I asked, hung up on this one fact.

Alice frowned. "Swimming with Kiera? She wanted to do a hair video with me, after ours went viral. No way I was going to, not after you told me that Halloween story."

"You're letting all the air out!" Alice's mom yelled from somewhere inside the house. Parents always knew when a door stayed open somewhere.

Alice closed the door behind her. "I figured that's why she egged my house."

I explained my theory that Kiera egged her house so that Alice wouldn't want to be friends with me anymore. I told her about my recent confrontation, embellishing a little so I sounded like a conquering hero. Okay, embellishing more than a little.

"Wow, Samira, I'm so impressed! And this time I won't even bulldoze you into an investigation to prove she did it."

We walked until we found a non-sticky spot to sit. "I'm sorry, Alice. About your house, your grandmother, everything."

"My grandmother is going to be okay." She scrunched her face and waved her hand in front of her nose. "And the smell will get better. I hope."

She sat cross-legged in the shade of a tree. "I wanted to come hang out with you guys. I thought I'd feel better with you and Umma and Imran. But when I figured out Kiera threw the eggs, I felt so awful. Kiera was getting back at me for not wanting to do a video with her, and now my grandmother is in the hospital." Alice hugged her knees. "Plus my mom wants us to move again before the school year starts. It's all too much."

"What?" Already I couldn't imagine the neighborhood without Alice. I sat next to her on the grass.

"She got another big job, all the way in Michigan. We have family there, and she wants to take Grandma with us. She doesn't want her to be alone."

A ladybug crawled across my leg. "Does your grand-mother want to move?" I asked.

"Not at all. Neither do I. Even with the egging and the toilet papering and the rude person at the grocery store and the mean girl in the neighborhood, I like it here."

I bounced my leg at the same speed as hers. "So that's

why you didn't text me back? I thought you were mad at me for egging your house!"

She pulled her phone from her back pocket. "What are you talking about? I did text you back." She showed me her responses, replies that had never reached my phone. "You really need a new phone, Samira."

"Wait, what about letting me still dance?" I asked, bobbing my head and turning my hands to re-create the moment.

She pumped her shoulders and turned the lightbulbs along with me. "That was entertainment gold. I wasn't going to stop you." I couldn't help but laugh.

"Your grandmother's not alone, you know. She has you, your mother, the whole neighborhood. Can't you convince your mom to stay?" I wasn't ready to say bye to Alice so soon. We fell into a silence, lost in our own thoughts.

An idea started to form. "Maybe if we can show your mom that you're not alone here, we could change her mind. About your grandmother moving. About you moving." My idea had a little more shape. "I think we should throw a party," I said.

"You? Samira? You think throwing a party is what we should do?"

I nodded. It was one of my better ideas.

"Wow, dancing in public really changed you, Samira." She elbowed me, wiggling her eyebrows. "So, how's this party supposed to change my life?" Alice asked.

I pulled some grass out of the ground and threw the blades at her. "Oh, you can't figure that out? Use your fancy powers of deduction?"

She threw grass back at me. "Oh, I don't have any." She stood to put some distance between us. "Once my grandmother was settled in at the hospital, she told my mom that Kiera threw the eggs. She saw her." She started to run. "That's how I knew." I chased after.

66

Body and Brain Catch-up

Imran straddled his bike, both feet on the ground, training wheels off. For two years I'd begged him to remove those extra wheels. I had stopped going on family bike rides because I didn't want to be seen with him and his training wheels.

"I'm teaching Umma how to ride a bike. Can you believe she doesn't know how?" Imran asked, ignoring the fact that he didn't either.

Umma stood next to Mom's bike, a loose grip on the handlebars, pallu of her saree tucked into her waist, ready for action. Hopefully not too much action. Two ambulances in two days would be two ambulances too many. A tragic tongue twister.

"Tell me again, Imran, how I'm supposed to do it?"

She lifted a foot to the pedal, and set it back down.

"You have to start pedaling right away, Umma, and fast."

He pushed one foot off the ground for speed and pedaled down the road. His front wheel was wobbly but moving. He dragged his feet to slow down before he turned around and pedaled back.

"Imran!" I said, recording his first ride. "You're doing it! You're riding on your own." No one could make Imran do anything until he was ready.

"Of course I am," he sighed, "Umma's the one who doesn't know how."

She wheeled the bike into the garage, leaning it against the wall. "Maybe I try later. I'm not fast learner like Imran."

"Probably right," Imran said. He turned to me and whispered, "She's hopeless."

"Now you and Dennis can ride bikes together when he comes," Umma said.

"Dennis?" I asked. As in the ruddy-faced friend of Leroy? But Umma was already heading back inside. "Who's Dennis, Imran?"

Imran practiced his pedaling. "You met Dennis. That day with Pete's band."

"He's coming over?" I asked. Imran was riding away, and I grabbed Mom's bike to catch up.

He turned his handlebars shakily, teetered but didn't fall.

"Yeah, he has a new Star Trek Lego set and wants to build it together."

I pedaled slowly to stay by his side. "You're friends with him?" I asked, trying to use my least preachy, least judgy voice.

"We've talked on the phone a few times," Imran said, casual, like he got phone calls from friends all the time. "He might even start coming to Mrs. Richardson's painting lessons."

I squeezed my handlebars in excitement for him but tried to play it cool. "What kind of things do you guys talk about?" I hadn't known seven-year-olds spent time on the phone. I never did.

"He talks a lot about Star Trek—"

"But you don't even like Star Trek," I said too quickly. I could have researched Star Trek words and binge-watched some episodes so Imran would know what to say.

He rode a perfect circle around me, his handlebars barely shaking. "Oh, I told him right away. He said that's fine. I still like building Legos."

I smiled for him. His first friend.

"Mom and Dad are going to be so excited you're riding

a bike on your own, Imran."

He hung his helmet on the wall when we got back. "Really?"

"Of course," I said, disbelief in my voice. "They've been trying to teach you for years."

What did he think they had been doing all those weekends?

"My brain always knew how to ride, Sammy. My body didn't want to until now."

I wondered if that was how Mom felt about me and all the debate clubs and speech clubs. Waiting for my brain and body to catch up. Waiting for me to speak up for myself.

"Umma," I yelled as we went back in the house. "I want to throw a big party." My arm was hooked around Imran's neck, dragging him inside.

"Like Umma big?" she asked.

"Bigger."

Party Hype Person

The three of us huddled around the kitchen table. Umma wasn't sure what to do with the pencil and notebook I had shoved into her hands, and Imran tinkered with a stack of Legos.

"Explain again, Samira, how big party will help Alice not move to Michigan?"

The idea had perfect clarity in my head, but blurred when I explained out loud. "Alice's mom wants to move everyone because she doesn't think they have enough people here to help. Not enough community," I explained. "I want to show them they do."

Imran stacked his bricks upside down like he always did, still magically building a skyscraper, or car, or airplane.

"You heard what Alice said at the dinner party, Umma." Was I pleading my case to Umma or to myself? "Her grandmother used to love those block parties. We're having a block party."

Umma traced the rose on the front of the notebook before opening it. "You know, Samira, Umma needs no excuse to throw a party."

"Oh, we know," Imran said. We all knew.

"But," she continued, her movements slow as she folded back the front cover, "maybe you expecting too much from party? I don't want you to be . . ."—she searched for the word—"disappointed."

All I knew was I needed to do something. Anything.

"I need to try, Umma."

She smoothed the page. "Okay. First we need location."

I wondered if it was possible to keep an Umma party simple. "How about right here?"

"Too many people," Imran said. He was building a helicopter, I think. "But they could probably fit in the backyard."

The backyard could work. "Perfect, Imran. Thank you." Also, my bedroom would be close enough if I needed to escape.

"Okay, when?" Umma asked.

"Alice's grandmother gets home the day after tomorrow," I said.

"Okay, we can do in two days." Umma could throw a wedding with two days' notice. I knew for a fact that she had. "What else we need?"

"Pete's band could play," Imran said, probably already planning the next song with us as backup.

I pulled him close and kissed him on the head. He didn't swat me away. "Imran, that's an excellent idea. Thank you! Thank you! I'll text Noor right now."

Me: Hey, Noor. Umma and I were thinking about doing a big block party day after tomorrow. Would you guys like to play?

Noor replied immediately: Okay but it will cost you

Me: How much

Noor: $1

Me: Deal.

Noor: Our first paying gig!!

I sent a thumbs-up emoji.

"We have a band!" Imran and Umma lifted their heads from their total focus on helicopters and menu planning.

"Excellent." Umma clapped her hands. "Now you need to let everyone know."

Knocking on more doors. Nightmare.

Imran flew his helicopter around, blowing out his cheeks to make sound effects, landing on the top of his building. "You could make a flyer, like Zaara did when she sold her T-shirts."

I pulled his head close again, but he pushed me away. "No more kissing, Sammy. I'm not kidding."

I backed off, hands in the air. "Okay, okay."

"Food," Umma said. "We need lots of food. I will make, of course, but put on flyer people can bring if they want."

"And decorations," Imran said, holding his hand to stop me from getting too close. "It's not a party without decorations."

"What should I call the party?" I asked, grabbing paper and uncapping markers, ready to create a flyer. Toilet papering, egging, Alice moving. "How about '(Worst)-Summer Block Party'?" I asked, shaping both my hands in curves to show the parentheses.

"Umm, no," Imran answered. Umma was already opening and shutting cupboards, taking inventory of what we had and what we needed.

"I was joking, Imran." I thought of Mrs. Richardson toilet papering her own front step for us, and Alice as my new friend, and Pete's band. "How about 'Best-Summer Block Party'?"

"That could work," he said, picking up markers to help color.

The next day we would have to spread the word, get people excited about the block party, get them to show up.

I was supposed to be the hype person. Who would have believed it? Not me.

Looking up an Elephant Butt

There was only one full day left before the party. The kitchen counters were covered with samosas draining on paper towels, dropped-off containers of pasta salad, and brownies covered with aluminum foil. Umma opened the fridge, shifting and stacking items to make room.

My feet hung over the arm of the couch, throbbing. Alice and I, sometimes with Imran, sometimes with Dennis, had walked up and down the neighborhood all day, dropping off flyers, picking up chairs and tables, borrowing strings of twinkle lights and paper lanterns and floor cushions. We had only asked for extra chairs, but every person had a different idea of what would make the perfect decoration, and we never said no.

Alice squeezed one foot, then the other, her legs crossed

under her. "I don't think there's any life left in them."
She meant her feet, but could have been talking about us.

"And we still have to decorate," I reminded her, weakly
lifting my finger to the mountain of things piled outside.
Fake plants and bolts of cloth had felt like an absolutely
necessary part of our decorations earlier that day.

She fell back, arms and legs splayed in a big X. "We
shouldn't have collected so much stuff. Why didn't you
stop me?"

I turned my feet in circles, slowing the throbbing.
"Stop you? I'm the one who thought the big white elephant was a fantastic idea." Its trunk was as high as our
heads and we had somehow lifted the front legs into the
wagon, pushing it like a strange wheelbarrow by its back
legs.

Alice giggled. "And the tail kept poking me in the eye."

"And I was looking straight up its butt," I laughed.
"The entire time."

Alice's giggle turned into a snort. She pretended to
poke her eye, like her finger was the elephant's tail. I
cupped my hands like a telescope and peered through,
pretending like I was looking up an elephant's butt. Her
laughter turned to hiccups. We lay there snorting and
roaring and hiccupping until we couldn't breathe.

"You girls having fun or I need to call doctor? I can't

tell," Umma yelled from the kitchen.

Which got us going all over again.

"We'd better get this done before it gets dark," I said, pulling Alice up by her outstretched hands.

We stood over our pile of decorations. Of course Alice took the elephant's tail and fake-poked her eye. Both of us fell to the ground immediately, laughter making it impossible to move.

"The band can use the deck as a stage," I said, surveying the backyard.

"Yeah, I was thinking the same. We can set up chairs there, and there," she gestured.

Neither of us had the energy or the right mood, but we went through the motions, and two hours later we stepped back to admire our work.

Pathetic. If I had to describe the decorations in one word.

Super pathetic. If I had two.

The chairs were lined up in uneven rows. Twinkle lights sagged like overstretched necklines on old T-shirts. Lanterns lay on the ground where we abandoned trying to hang them. Red floor cushions dotted the grass, reminding me of acne sprouting overnight on my forehead. Plastic flowers drooped from backs of chairs. I hadn't known plastic flowers could even droop.

Umma dusted her hands as she checked on us, a flour cloud around her. "How are you girls doing?" she asked, in case it wasn't obvious. We drooped like our decorations. "Looks . . . umm . . . comfortable," she added.

"Comfortable" wasn't the look we were going for.

"You need help?" Umma asked, shaking her phone in front of her. "Secret weapon ready to go."

We were supposed to do this ourselves. A strand of pink streamer taped to the sliding door fell loose and landed on Umma's head.

"I think we might need it," Alice answered.

Umma was already punching numbers into her phone. "It's okay to ask for help, Samira. You ask for help. I ask for help. People like to help."

"I guess," I said, catching another falling streamer.

"I tell help to come tomorrow," Umma said, ushering us inside, where much-needed plates of chapati and chicken stew waited on the counter.

The Secret Weapon Plus Me

"Catch the end of this, would you, Joe?" a woman yelled from the top of a ladder leaning against our patio door.

I had thought I was sneaking downstairs early, hoping to secretly cut off a slice of something sweet and sticky from the many options on the counters, still rubbing the sleep from my eyes.

My reflection on the patio door showed how my curls stuck out at all angles and my pajama pants were too short. The glass was cool against my forehead and I shaded my eyes to see outside. A roll of lights tumbled down and I couldn't help but make eye contact with the man holding the bottom of the ladder. I didn't recognize him, but we were separated by only a pane of glass, so I waved. He smiled, not letting go of the ladder.

Imran was dancing around Mrs. Richardson as she looped gold net over the back of chairs. Gone were the pimple-floor cushions, saggy-T-shirt lights, uneven rows of chairs. Alice waved, both hands full with streamers in pink and purple she was weaving together into strands.

Umma had deployed her amazing, never-fail, internationally effective secret weapon.

I waited for the woman to come down from the ladder before stepping outside. Another awkward wave. Another smile.

The backyard was bustling. Some people I knew from the neighborhood, and some I didn't. Tables lined both sides of the yard, covered in bright pink and yellow. The deck had a ceiling of twinkle lights, and candles of different heights formed a border for the stage. Lanterns hung from tree branches and poles stuck in the ground, and cushions were pushed together in threes and fours on small rugs of different patterns. I recorded all of it. For Mom and Dad. For me.

Alice pulled apart the streamers to show off the basket pattern she had made. "Isn't it gorgeous?" she asked.

"Yes, it is," I said, still taking it all in. "My grandmother is absolutely amazing."

Mrs. Richardson handed me a piece of cloth. "Your grandmother is amazing for sure," she said, showing me how to twist the material over the back of the chair. "But this, Samira,"—she opened her arms wide to take in the backyard—"is not her doing."

"I've got the smoke machine up and running," Mr. Carter yelled to no one in particular.

Imran jumped to catch a runaway balloon, not quite tall enough to rescue it from the lowest branches of a tree.

"All of this, Samira," Mrs. Richardson said, "is because of you."

The balloon escaped, floating away with a long red ribbon tail trailing behind.

My Shield and Hers

I rubbed the back of my neck where it ached from crouching over what felt like a hundred little candles, checking their batteries. Their flicker was real, the flame was not.

"Hi." I heard the familiar voice and my shoulders froze. I wondered if she had brought Kiera with her. I stood up in the tight circle of the candles, careful to not knock any over even though they weren't real.

Mrs. Carter stopped to pull her heel out of the ground, and Kiera trailed behind her. "Oh, Sammy," she said, still making her way over, doing a strange tip toe when her heel sunk into the grass again. "I know you're setting up for your big party, but I was hoping to talk to your grandmother." The candles stopped her from coming closer. "I fear there's been a misunderstanding."

Kiera chewed her lower lip and adjusted her bangs to cover her eyes.

"About what?" I asked, not finishing the sentence with her name.

She tilted her head. "About what, *Mrs. Carter*?" She put her hands on her hips, drumming her fingers. I didn't repeat the words.

"Maybe you want to run a comb through your hair. This is not how we receive guests, is it, Sammy?"

I patted my hair from below, poofing the curls more.

Umma materialized outside the ring of candles, but still close. "Yes?" she asked with no smile on her face or in her voice.

Kiera's mom pointed a finger, her bright red nail inches from Umma's nose. "I need to talk to you about your granddaughter," she said. Umma stood her ground until Mrs. Carter was forced to put away her finger.

"Always happy to talk about my grandchildren. My favorite topic," Umma answered. Mrs. Carter hadn't come over for a cup of tea and casual conversation about how cute I was. The way Umma's jaw clenched meant she knew exactly what Mrs. Carter was doing.

"Sammy has accused my daughter of throwing eggs at her friend's house. You understand how serious this accusation is, don't you?" She tapped her nails across her phone screen, the sound of a horse trotting.

"It's true, Umma," I said. Alice stepped carefully, avoiding knocking over candles until she stood in my circle.

"Ridiculous," Kiera said, still biting her lip.

"Ridiculous," her mother echoed, and her tapping sped to a gallop. "Now her friends aren't talking to her. We need Sammy to straighten this out. We demand an apology."

Imran came running out of the house, almost knocking over Mrs. Carter. "Hey, Kiera's mom. Hey, Kiera." Always oblivious. "Did you bring banana bread for the party?" I winced when he landed on my foot after leaping over the candles in a single bound, not wearing a cape when finally it could have made sense. He understood on which side of the candles he belonged.

Imran, Alice, Umma. They were my shield.

"Better we speak privately. Don't you agree?" Umma asked, her arm directing Mrs. Carter to the deck. She stopped clacking her nails, dropped her phone in her purse, and followed Umma.

Alice pressed her shoulder against mine, the three of us standing in our circle, Kiera on the outside. We could hear bits of the conversation between Umma and Mrs. Carter. Umma's voice was steady. Mrs. Carter's voice decreased in volume and anger the more they spoke.

"You can't just say whatever you want without any proof," Kiera said to me and my shield.

I had thought I wanted to prove Kiera's toilet papering and egging.

I had thought I needed the proof.

Instead I learned that when people know you well enough, you don't have to prove anything.

Alice stepped forward; one candle fell over, knocking the next one and the next. "She doesn't need proof, Kiera. My grandmother saw you throwing the eggs."

Kiera blinked. "There's no—" she started to say, but stopped. "This is ridiculous," she said, reaching for the same word she had used earlier. She walked to her mom, pulling on her purse, interrupting whatever Umma was saying. "Let's go home."

With three long strides, Kiera's grandfather joined them. I had my shield and they had theirs. "What's going on?" he asked.

"We're talking about how Kiera egged Alice's house, but she was going to apologize, right Kiera?" Umma said, speaking without anger, like the accusation was now widely accepted fact.

"You egged her house, Kiera?" her grandfather asked.

"Let's go home," Kiera's mom said, with none of her necklace-pulling, phone-clacking bravado.

We exited our circle through the path of toppled candles. "She also toilet papered the tree in front of my house," I said.

"That's ridiculous," Mrs. Carter said. The word had lost all meaning. "My daughter is not some sort of delinquent."

Half the decorators and light-hangers acted like they were working, ears perked. The other half gave up all pretense, arms limp by their sides, full attention on us.

Mr. Carter held his index finger up, telling Kiera's mom to wait a moment. "Is this true, Kiera?"

She shook her head no.

"Of course it's not—" Mrs. Carter started to say before her father quieted her again.

He paused in thought. "Is that why you took the T-shirt cannon from our house that night, Kiera?" Mr. Carter asked. "To launch toilet paper? Is it?" he repeated when Kiera stayed quiet. "I was wondering why you were suddenly so interested in my old job at the stadium." He sounded exhausted.

"But Sammy—" she started.

"I'm sorry for the disruption, everyone," Mr. Carter said to us. "I think it's time for us to leave."

"But Sammy," Kiera tried to say again.

He led them away, to the front of the house. "I believe she goes by Samira now."

71

Twinkle-Light Perfection

"Shall we do a trial run before all the guests arrive?" I had the stage to myself while Imran, Umma, and Alice were the sole audience members.

We had washed off the backyard grime, changed out of our grass-stained, sweaty clothes, and Alice was back, dressed in head-to-toe fluorescent pink. "Wow," Imran said to her, "you look like a highlighter." He was trying to say the nicest thing he could think of.

Lights, sound, sturdiness of tables, coziness of seating: everything had been checked, and the four of us were left alone. "Do we need a countdown?" I asked, crouching to reach the plug point behind the barbecue grill.

"Three!" Imran yelled.

"Two," Umma said, holding up two fingers.

"One!" Alice was practically squealing.

I fumbled on all fours, wiggling the plug one way and the other before it fell into place.

The way Umma's mouth opened, and Imran's eyes widened, and Alice put both hands on her face, I knew the stage was perfect.

Pete, Billy, and Noor arrived exactly when the last of the work was complete, carrying boxes and bags I was familiar with from my roadie duties.

Noor was wearing a shimmering dress of black mesh, over camouflage pants. "Wow! You're amazing, Umma."

"Not me," Umma said, waving her hand in front of her like she was swatting away the idea. "Samira and Alice."

"Well, mostly Samira," Alice said.

"No, mostly Alice," I said back to her, still standing onstage. "And the whole neighborhood came to help."

"Mostly me," Imran yelled, jumping off a chair.

"Well, whoever it was, this is beautiful," Pete said. You don't need to strum your first note to find your smile when there are twinkle lights.

I stepped off the stage to see things from their view. The deck was absolutely transformed. Little white lights glowed above, all the candles on the ground were lit— every single battery checked. I turned a full circle to take it all in—chairs were draped in blue and green velvet, Mrs. Richardson's paintings and mobiles in bright pinks and greens added color everywhere, chalk swirls and flowers had been drawn on the ground in rangoli patterns. Tables flanked either side of the lawn, covered with real and fake flowers, Lego characters, and streamer garlands.

The only way it could have been more perfect was if the rest of the family were there. My phone buzzed.

72

The Final Video

All three of them were squeezed into the frame, to see and be seen.

"Show us everything." Mom adjusted the phone so I wasn't looking up their noses.

I walked around the yard, taking them on a tour, enjoying their wows and oohs and aahs.

Zaara pushed Mom's head down so she could see better. "Sammy, you did so good!"

I had been planning to wait a few more days, until they got back, to tell them, but I couldn't. "I kind of prefer Samira now. What do you think?" I added, with a nervous laugh.

"I love it," Dad said. Passing traffic honked outside their window. "You've been Samira to us all along."

Mrs. Markley was the first to arrive. She wasn't part of

our neighborhood, but I had invited her because there was something special I wanted to share.

"It's going to get loud soon," I said to the three of them on my phone. Pete was already fiddling with his guitar onstage, "but I have a surprise. I can't wait for you to see."

I balanced my phone against the crate of orange soda and Thums Up, turning it one way and the other until Mom, Dad, and Zaara could see the stage.

More people arrived, one carrying their baby, another holding their dog leash. I wanted to do this before the place really filled up. I wasn't ready for prime time yet.

"Umm," I said, standing in front of the stage, but Umma was on the other side of the yard, too far to hear me. "Excuse me," I said a little louder, but she was busy welcoming people, directing them to food, explaining the rangoli. If I didn't do this quickly, I'd lose my nerve. I climbed the few steps to the deck/stage. "Hello, everyone." My voice boomed through the microphone and across the yard. "I made a video. I wanted to play it for everyone, especially my grandmother. Sorry and thank you." This video was the one I wanted her to remember. I wanted her to know this was how I really felt about her. I had practiced saying all of that. But the lights were distracting, and I hadn't been expecting others to be there already, and I had to do it before I backed out.

I started the video on my laptop, the video I had worked on late into the night, and was still editing five minutes before the party. The sound was barely audible, and I wasn't sure Umma could see my screen from across the yard. Mrs. Markley set her drink down and made her way to me.

"May I, Samira?" she asked, plugging in my computer to the boxes and wires we had set up for the band. "So excited to see this. So excited you're sharing."

A picture of me projected to the big white sheet that hung behind the stage as a makeshift screen, paused on the center of my nose before Mrs. Markley resumed the video. I had edited the whole thing down to three minutes. "The submission was meant to be three separate videos," video-me said. The screen was wrinkled and my nose looked crooked. "As much as I edited and took new shots and changed background music, I couldn't make the videos feel genuine to me." In the background of the video, one of my birthday bears fell off the window. "I realized that I couldn't separate the three. Home, community, world. For me, all three start with my grandmother, my Umma."

I had chosen my grandfather's favorite Mohammed Rafi song, and I saw Umma sit down when she heard the first piano notes. I sat with her. The video started with shots from around the house of Umma in the kitchen, the three of us in front of Imran's blanket fort, Umma with her saree tucked in her waist playing soccer in the backyard. I had clips of all of us in Pete's band shimmying and singing, everyone gathered around Umma's dinner table laughing and eating, Mrs. Richardson with the painting she made for Umma, short videos of people on ladders and unfurling tablecloths to set up the backyard. I ended with shots of my toilet papered tree, beautiful shots of blurry leaves and light streaming through branches. Umma squeezed my hand tighter and tighter.

I had wanted to write something at the end, even chose the font and size of the letters, but everything sounded silly.

"Thank you" was too little.

"I love you" was too obvious.

"I'm sorry for the last video" was too embarrassing.

So I wrote nothing.

But Umma knew what I meant. She always did.

Guests gathered around, telling her how much they loved the video, and Umma never missed a chance to brag about me.

"That was beautiful," Mrs. Markley said, "I loved every second."

I unplugged my laptop and started to put things away, happy to have something to occupy me, embarrassed by the attention.

"You didn't even follow the submission rules, Sammy," Imran said. "So you're probably not going to win." Like he ever followed any rules.

"I know," I said, dropping my laptop into its sleeve. "It was more important to me that the video felt right. Mrs. Markley taught me that." She beamed at me.

"My favorite shots were the dinner party ones," Alice said. "And I loved that you included the toilet papered tree."

I didn't mind talking about the toilet papering anymore. "If it wasn't for the tree, maybe none of this would have happened," I said. And I really did believe that.

Homecoming

P eople filtered in, old and new friends eating together, making themselves comfortable on the floor cushions. The band finished warming up and started to play.

Alice pulled me by my arm. "They're here! My mom and grandmother are here from the hospital." We both ran around the house to the driveway where their car was idling. Her grandmother sat in the back. She wore bright red glasses and had brilliantly white hair, cut super short. I hadn't seen her grandmother in years. She looked a lot older than I remembered. Alice opened the car door and threw herself on her grandmother. I stood by clumsily, waiting for them to let go.

"Sounds like quite the party back there," Alice's mother said, smiling as she checked the rearview mirror to see Alice and her grandmother still stuck together.

"It's a welcome home party," I said.

Alice and her grandmother finally separated. "It is, Grandma. This whole party is for you."

"For me?" her grandmother said. Her voice was so soft and gentle, you knew she kept hard candy in her purse, and always had chocolate cake under a dome in her kitchen.

"You have to come see," Alice said, stepping out of the car to take them to the back and show them. "The whole neighborhood is here to say hello. This was all Samira's idea." There was cheering in the backyard when the song ended. Maybe because the song had ended.

Alice's mom turned the car off. "You girls did a wonderful job. Amazing," her grandmother said. "And Samira, we never believed even for a minute that you were the one who egged our house."

"Mom," Alice said, "you should have seen Samira confront Kiera. In front of grown-ups and everything. Kiera couldn't say a single word by the end." I hoped I didn't sound like a bully. "I think she might come by to say sorry." The sound of Noor's drums drifted over to us before Pete and Billy joined in.

Alice's mom got out of the car. "And I wouldn't hesitate to accept her apology. We've all done things we regret. I'm sure she will learn to make better choices."

The microphone screeched from the backyard. If I were there, I would know how to fix it. I didn't need to forgive her and never wanted to be her friend again, but it would be nice if she went back to being the old Kiera.

"Okay, Grandma," Alice said, "time to make your grand entrance."

Alice's mom leaned into the car and stroked her cheek. "Honey, getting your grandmother into the car and the drive over has really worn her out. She needs to get home to rest. I don't think we could get her wheelchair to the backyard anyway."

Alice tugged at her mom's shirt, like a little kid. "But you have to see. We have people here too. We don't have to move to Michigan."

Her mom pulled her into a hug and kissed her cheek. "That's what this is about?"

"I like it here, Mom. I like living with Grandma. I don't want to keep moving."

Her mom's face crumpled. "I thought you said you didn't mind moving so much?"

"I do now," Alice said. She lifted her face from her mom's chest, leaving behind an imprint in makeup of red lips and blue eyes.

"Why don't we talk it out tomorrow? You go have fun right now."

Alice's grandmother leaned through the window. "I'll tell you something. There's no way in hell I'm moving anywhere at all." Which made Alice laugh.

"Mom, the cursing!" her mom said.

"I'm glad you're going to stay at the party," I said as their car backed out. Without her, I wasn't sure I could handle all the conversations with people I barely knew. "I really hope you don't have to move. Do you think we did enough?"

"I hope so," Alice said, "I love having my best friend right down the street."

Everything's Perfect Right Here

"The next song," Pete said, taking on full rock star persona, as if the audience was thousands in a stadium instead of the thirty or forty people holding paper plates of kebabs and brownies. "The next song is dedicated to a special person. Someone who made all this possible."

Please don't say my name, I begged in my head, plastering on a strained smile in case they did. They could mean Alice. They could mean Umma. They could even mean Kiera, since toilet paper was the beginning and the eggs were the end. Just please don't say my name.

"Samira." He confirmed my fears. "Come on up."

My whole body tightened, but somehow I managed to raise my hand, bent at the elbow, and wave with small turns. Apparently I was the queen of England.

"Nope, you're coming up here," Pete said, curling his finger to summon me. "We know you have it in you."

In the back of Mrs. Richardson's garage, with an audience of exactly zero, sure. I pointed to the food on my plate and then my mouth. The queen needed her samosa.

Pete put both hands on his hips, his guitar hanging in front. "Samira, get up here."

"You'd better go," Alice said, pointing to the stage with her fork, her words making my mouth immediately dry. I coughed up samosa.

"Samira." Pete's voice boomed loud and low into the microphone. What if everyone started to chant my name? Or worse, they started that slow clap.

I put both our plates down and grabbed Alice's hand, pulling her with me, painfully aware of the strange quiet as everyone stopped talking, eating, and throwing beanbags into holes. All eyes were on us as we made our way to the stage. Imran stuck out his bright blue tongue as we walked past, and I grabbed his arm. I wasn't going down alone.

Umma and Mrs. Richardson had their heads tilted back in laughter, sharing Mrs. Richardson's famous chocolate chip cookies and a joke, unaware of my discomfort.

"Imran," I whispered, "grab them too."

Imran was always happy to volunteer others without their permission, and took Umma's hand.

"You, too, Mrs. Richardson," I said.

We formed an unlikely, wobbly chain, walking to the makeshift stage.

"So what will it be?" Pete asked.

I looked to my left, where Umma, Mrs. Richardson, and Imran stood giggling, ready to perform any song. I looked to my right, and I was still holding Alice's hand even though I never had to drag her to do anything with me. She was always there.

"I think you know," I told Pete.

He pretended to clutch his chest in pain.

The opening intro was unmistakable, catching everyone's attention. Soon the whole audience would be singing along, pumping fists, or at the very least, tapping their feet.

"There's room for one person on stage. Come on up, Samira."

I'm not the front-of-stage sort of person. "Thank you, but no," I answered, shaking my head. I was learning to tell people what I wanted and what I didn't.

Umma knocked me with her swaying hips, Alice grabbed my hand, and Imran accidentally stepped on my foot.

"Things are perfect right here."

Acknowledgments

I was just coming to terms with the fact that I have a book out in the world, and now I'm lucky enough to do it all over again. I'm not exaggerating when I say Alyssa Henkin is the best agent in the entire universe. Thank you for making all this a reality.

To Alex Cooper, thank you for (so gently) helping me find my way to a story, for seeing the big picture and the tiny details at the same time, and for making this stronger and oh so much better.

Thank you to Allison Weintraub for your insight and all your help, and for my favorite tagline ever.

To David DeWitt, David Curtis, and Chaaya Prabhat, thank you for this gorgeous, can't-look-away cover. To Jennifer Sale, Vinny Cusenza, Rye White, and Mikayla Lawrence, thank you for being kind when correcting tense and removing commas. To Rosemary Brosnan and the entire team at Quill Tree and HarperCollins, including Gwen Morton, Allison Brown, Lauren Levite, Nicole Wills, Sabrina Abballe, and Patty Rosati and her team, thank you, thank you.

I know finding the perfect writing group is equal parts luck and alchemy. Jonathan Bing, Kara Thom, and Jon

Wallace, without you three I would still be staring at a blank document on my laptop. I'm so grateful to The Inkslayers for making me comfortable enough to share that very rough first draft, for the immeasurable help and guidance, for Nobodies, for poetry, for wraiths, and for friendship. I harpoon all of you!

To my OG writing community—Nigar Alam. I'm grateful you're smart enough to answer all my questions and patient enough to do it repeatedly. Thank you, friend.

It's no surprise both of my books include strong teachers. I think teachers are everything. My children want to thank their favorites: Mr. Boberg, Ms. Duncan, Mrs. Ikola, and Sr. Storlie.

There are people (and pieces of furniture) who don't know I exist but helped me get unstuck when I was stuck. Julia Louis-Dreyfus and her podcast, Chef Ann Kim on Netflix, and Room & Board's cozy swivel chair.

And, of course, a big thank-you to my parents, and to Minoo, Muna, Khurshid, Hana, Sofie, Omar, Ayesha, and Adam for making everything better and everything worthwhile.